THE D·I·S·T·A·N·C·E BETWEEN US

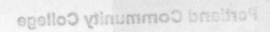

THE D·I·S·T·A·N·C·E BETWEEN US

KASIE WEST

HARPER TEEN
An Imprint of HarperCollinsPublishers

HarperTeen is an imprint of HarperCollins Publishers.

The Distance Between Us
Copyright © 2013 by Kasie West

Library of Congress Cataloging-in-Publication Data is available.
West, Kasie.
The distance between us / Kasie West. — First edition.
    pages cm
Summary: "Seventeen-year-old Caymen Meyers knows better than
to trust a rich boy. But then she meets the richest guy of all, who proves
money might not matter after all"— Provided by publisher.
ISBN 978-0-06-223565-7 (pbk.)
[1. Dating (Social customs)—Fiction. 2. Wealth—Fiction. 3. Single-
parent families—Fiction. 4. Mothers and daughters—Fiction.] I. Title.
PZ7.W51837Dis 2013   2013003173
[Fic]—dc23   CIP
                                                                  AC

Typography by Torborg Davern
13 14 15 16 17 LP/RRDH 10 9 8 7 6 5 4 3 2 1
❖
First Edition

THE D·I·S·T·A·N·C·E BETWEEN US

CHAPTER 1

. . . .

My eyes burn a hole in the page. I should know this. I can usually dissect a science equation easily, but the answer isn't coming to me. The bell on the door dings. I quickly tuck my homework beneath the counter and look up. A guy on a cell phone walks in.

That's new.

Not the cell phone part but the guy part. It isn't that men don't frequent the doll store— Okay, actually it is. Men don't frequent the store. They are a rare sighting. When they do come in, they trail behind feminine types and look extremely self-conscious . . . or bored. This one is neither. He's very much alone and confident. The kind of confidence only money can buy. Lots of it.

I smile a little. There are two types of people in our small beach town: the rich and the people who sell things to the rich. Apparently having money means collecting useless things like porcelain dolls (the adjective "useless" should never be used around my mother when referring to dolls). The rich are our constant entertainment.

"What do you mean you want *me* to pick?" Mr. Rich says into the phone. "Didn't Grammy tell you which one she wanted?" He lets out a long sigh. "Fine. I'll take care of it." He pockets his phone and beckons me over. Yes. Beckons. It's the only word I can use to describe the motion. He hadn't even glanced my way but held up his hand and moved two fingers in his direction. His other hand rubs his chin while he studies the dolls in front of him.

I size him up as I walk over. The untrained eye might not pick up on the richness oozing off this guy, but I know rich and he reeks of it. His one outfit probably cost more than all the clothes in my tiny closet. Not that it looks expensive. It's an outfit that's purposefully trying to downplay how much it cost: a pair of cargo pants, a pink button-down rolled at the sleeves. But the clothes were purchased somewhere that specializes in thread count and triple stitching. It's obvious he can buy the whole store if he wants to. Well, not him; his parents. I didn't realize it at first because his confidence aged him, but now that I'm closer I can see he's young. My age maybe? Seventeen. Although he could be a year older. How is someone my age already so versed at beckoning? A lifetime of privilege, obviously.

"Can I help you, sir?" Only my mom would've heard the sarcasm laced into that single statement.

"Yes, I need a doll."

"Sorry, we're all out." A lot of people don't get my humor. My mom calls it dry humor. I think that means "not funny," but it also means I'm the only one who ever knows it's a joke. Maybe if I laugh afterward, like my mom does when she's helping customers, more people would humor me, but I can't bring myself to do it.

"Funny," he says, but not like he actually thinks it's funny; more like he wishes I wouldn't talk at all. He still hasn't looked at me. "So which one of these do you think an older woman might like?"

"All of them."

The muscle in his jaw jumps and then he turns toward me. For a split second I see surprise in his eyes, like he expected some old woman to be standing in front of him—I blame my voice, which is slightly deeper than average—but it doesn't stop him from saying the sentence already spilling over his lips: "Which one do you like?"

Am I allowed to say "none"? Despite the fact it's my inevitable future, the store is my mom's love, not mine. "I'm partial to the eternal wailers."

"Excuse me?"

I point to the porcelain version of a baby, his mouth open in a silent cry, his eyes squeezed shut. "I'd rather not see their eyes. Eyes can say so much. Theirs say, 'I want to steal your soul so don't turn your back on us.'"

I'm rewarded with a smile that takes away all the hard, arrogant edges on his face, leaving him very attractive. He should definitely make that a permanent fixture. But before I even finish the thought, the smile's gone.

"My grammy's birthday is coming up and I'm supposed to pick out a doll for her."

"You can't go wrong. If she likes porcelain dolls, she'll like any of them."

He looks back at the shelves of dolls. "Why the wailers? Why not the sleepers?" He's staring at a peaceful-looking baby, a pink bow in her blond curls, her hands tucked under her cheek, her face relaxed.

I stare at her, too, and contrast her to the wailer next to her. The one whose fists are balled, its toes curled, its cheeks pink with irritation. "Because that's my life: screaming without making a sound." Okay, so I didn't really say that. I thought it. What I really say after a shrug is "They both work." Because if I've learned anything about customers it's that they don't really want your opinion. They want you to tell them their opinion is valid. So if Mr. Rich wants the sleeping baby for *Grammy*, who am I to stop him?

He shakes his head as if eradicating a thought and then points to a completely different shelf occupied by dolls of the soul-sucking variety. The girl he points to is dressed in a plaid school uniform and holds the leash of a black Scottish terrier. "I guess that one will work. She likes dogs."

"Who does? Your grandma or"—I squint to read the placard in front of the doll—"Peggy?"

"It's quite obvious Peggy likes dogs," he says, a hint of a smile playing on his lips. "I was referring to my grandmother."

I open the lower cupboard to find Peggy's box. I pull it out and gently take the girl and her dog, along with her name placard, off the shelf and to the register. As I carefully pack her away, Mr. Rich points. "How come the dog isn't named?" He reads aloud the title on the box. "'Peggy and *dog*.'"

"Because people tend to want to name animals after their beloved pets."

"Really?"

"No. I have no idea. I can give you the number of Peggy's creator if you want to ask."

"You have the phone number of this doll's creator?"

"No." I punch the price into the register and push Total.

"You're hard to read," he says.

Why is he trying to read *me*? We were talking about dolls. He hands me a credit card and I swipe it through the machine. The name on the card says, "Xander Spence." Xander as in "Z-ander" or as in "X-ander"? I'm not going to ask. I really don't care. I've been pleasant enough. This exchange wouldn't even have required a mom-lecture, had she been here. My mom is way better at hiding her resentment than I am. She even hides it from me. I chalk it up to years of practice.

His cell phone rings and he takes it out of his pocket. "Hello?"

While I wait for the machine to spit out his slip, I open the drawer beneath the register and put the name placard along with the others sold this month. This helps us remember which dolls we need to reorder.

"Yes, I found one. It has a dog." He listens for a minute. "No. *It's* not a dog. It *has* a dog. The doll has a dog." He turns around the box and looks at the picture of Peggy since the real Peggy is secured inside. "I guess she's cute." He looks at me and shrugs as though asking if I agree. I nod. Peggy is definitely cute. "Yes, it's been confirmed by the salesgirl. *She's* cute."

I know he wasn't talking about me being cute, but the

way he emphasized the "she" made it sound like he was. I look down and rip off the paper then hold a pen out for him to sign. He does it one-handed, and I compare the signature to the one on the card then hand it back to him.

"No, not the . . . I mean she is, too, but . . . Oh you know what I mean. It's fine. I'll be home soon." He sighs. "Yes, I mean *after* the bakery. Remind me to run away when your assistant has a day off." He squeezes his eyes shut. "I didn't mean it like that. Yes, of course it makes me appreciate things more. Okay, Mom, I'll see you soon. Bye."

I hand him the bagged doll.

"Thanks for your help."

"No problem."

He picks up a business card from the holder by the register and studies it for a moment. "'And more'?"

The name of the store is Dolls and More. He's asking what others have before him once they come into the store and only see dolls. I nod. "Dolls and *more* dolls."

He tilts his head.

"We used to carry charm bracelets and stuffed animals and such, but the dolls got jealous."

He gives me a look that seems to say, *Are you for real?* Obviously he has never encountered anyone like me in any of his "go visit the common people so you can appreciate your life more" outings. "Let me guess, the dolls threatened to steal your soul if you didn't comply with their demands."

"No, they threatened to release the souls of past customers. We couldn't have that."

He laughs, which surprises me. I feel like I earned something not many others have, and I smile despite myself.

I nod my head toward the card. "My mom likes dolls the best. She got tired of stocking stuffed mice." Plus we could no longer afford the extras. Something had to go and it wasn't going to be the dolls. And since we are in a perpetual state of broke (as in barely enough money to stay afloat), the name of the store and business cards stayed the same.

He jams a finger at the card. "Susan? That's your mom?"

And that's all it says, too, her first name followed by the shop's phone number, like she's some stripper or something. I cringe when she hands out a business card outside of the store. "Yes, sir."

"And you are?" He meets my eyes.

"Her daughter." I know he's asking for my name, but I don't want to give it. The first thing I learned about the rich is that they find the common folk an amusing distraction but would never, *ever* want anything real. And that's fine with me. The rich are another type of species that I observe only from a safe distance. I don't interact with them.

He replaces the card and takes a few steps backward. "Do you know where Eddie's Bakery is?"

"It's two blocks that way. Be careful. Their blueberry muffins are laced with some sort of addictive substance."

He nods. "Noted."

CHAPTER 2

● ● ● ● ● ● ●

"No, we don't carry Barbie dolls, only porcelain dolls," I say into the phone for the fifth time. The woman isn't listening. She's going off about how her daughter will die if she can't find the faerie queen. "I understand. Maybe you should try Walmart."

"I did. They're out." She mumbles something about how she thought we were a doll store and hangs up.

I set the phone down and roll my eyes at Skye, who doesn't notice because she's lying on the floor holding her necklace in the air, watching it sway back and forth over her.

Skye Lockwood is my one and only friend. Not because the kids at my high school are mean or anything. They just forget I exist. When I leave before lunch and never attend their social gatherings it's not hard to do.

Skye is a few years older and works next door at a place that carries lots of "and more." It's an antique store called Hidden Treasures that I call Obvious Garbage. But people love that store.

In the world of science, if Skye were a host, I would be her parasite. She has a life. I pretend it's mine. In other words, she genuinely likes things—music and eclectic vintage clothing and weird hairstyles—and I pretend those things interest me, too. It's not that I hate those things; it's just that I don't really care for them either. But I like Skye, so why not tag along? Especially because I have no idea what I really do like.

I step over her with a sigh. "Have you figured out life's answers yet?" Skye often uses the floor of the shop to have philosophical wanderings (a fancy way of saying "arguments with herself").

She moans and throws her arm over her eyes. "What would I even study if I went to college?" If it were up to her, she'd work at the gift store forever, but college is important to her never-went-to-college-so-is-now-a-funeral-director father.

"Whining?"

"Ha-ha." She pushes herself to sitting. "What are you going to study when you go?"

No idea. "The long-term effects of philosophical wanderings."

"How about the art of sarcasm?"

"I'm pretty sure I've already earned the equivalent of a master's in that one."

"No, but seriously, what are you going to study?"

I hear those words a lot: "No, but seriously" or "In all seriousness" or "But really." Those are the words of someone who wants a real answer. And I don't want to give one.

"I haven't thought about it much. I guess I'll be one of those 'no major' people for a while."

She lies back down. "Yeah, maybe that's what I'll do, too. Maybe as we take classes our true path will come to us." She sits up suddenly with a gasp.

"What?"

"We should take classes together! Next year. You and me. That would be awesome!"

I've told her a million times I'm not taking college classes next year. My mother will fight this plan (which is why I haven't told her), but I'm taking a year or two off so I can help full-time in the store. But Skye looks so happy that I just smile and give a noncommittal nod.

She starts singing a made-up song. "Me and Caymen

takin' classes together. Finding our true paths . . ." Her voice gets softer and turns into happy humming as she lowers herself back to the floor.

A couple of little girls who just left had touched everything. My mom insists that when people know a doll's name, it's easier to fall in love with it. So in front of every doll is a placard. Now those little name cards are completely messed up, switched around, lying flat. It's really sad that I know Bethany's name card is in front of Susie. Really. Really. Sad.

Skye's phone rings. "Hello? . . . No. I'm at The Little Shop of Horrors." That's what she calls my store.

It's quiet for a while before she says, "I didn't realize you were coming by." She stands and leans against the counter. "You did? When?" She twists a piece of hair around her finger. "Well, I am kind of spaced out during that show." Skye's voice matches her name, light and airy, which makes everything that comes out of her mouth sound sweet and innocent. "So are you still here?" She walks around doll cradles and blanket-draped tables to the front window and peers out. "I see you. . . . I'm next door at the doll store. Come over." She pockets the phone.

"Who was that?"

"My boyfriend."

"The boyfriend. So does this mean I finally get to meet him?"

She smiles. "Yes, you're about to see why I said yes the second he asked me out last week." She flings open the front door, and the bell practically swings off its hook. "Hey, baby."

He wraps his arms around her and then she moves aside. "Caymen, this is Henry. Henry, Caymen."

I don't know if I'm not looking hard enough, but I definitely don't *see* much of anything. He's scrawny with long greasy hair and a pointy nose. A pair of sunglasses hangs off the collar of a band T-shirt, and a long chain attached to his belt buckle droops halfway down his leg before disappearing into his back pocket. Without meaning to I calculate how many steps it took him to get from Skye's store to mine and how many times that chain must've hit him in the leg.

"S'up?" he says. Really. He said that.

"Um . . . nothing?"

Skye gives me a wide smile that says, *See, I knew you'd love him*. The girl can find redeeming qualities in a drowned rat, but I'm still trying to make sense of the match-up. Skye is beautiful. Not the conventional beautiful. In fact people usually stop to stare first because they're stunned by her choppy blond hair with pink tips, the diamond stud in her chin, and her crazy clothes. But then they keep staring because she's stunning, with her piercing blue eyes and the most beautiful bone structure ever.

Henry is now turning a circle, looking at all the dolls. "Whoa, trippy."

"I know, right? It's a little overwhelming the first time."

I look around. It *is* a little overwhelming at first. Dolls cover nearly every inch of wall in an explosion of colors and expressions. All staring at us. Not only the walls, but the floor space is a maze of tables and cradles and strollers overflowing with dolls. In case of fire there is no clear exit to the door. I'd be pushing babies out of the way to escape. Fake babies, but still.

Henry walks up to a doll wearing a kilt. "Aislyn," he says, reading her name card. "I have this outfit. I should get this doll and we can go on tour together."

"Playing bagpipes?" I ask.

He gives me a funny look. "Nope. I'm the guitar player for Crusty Toads."

Ah, and there it is. The reason Skye keeps him around. She has a soft spot for musicians. But she can do much better than a guy who looks like he was the inspiration for his band's name.

"Die, you ready?"

"Yep."

Die? I'll ask her about that later.

"See you later, Caveman," he says with a guffaw like

he'd been saving that up since the second we were introduced.

I wouldn't need to ask about Die, after all. He's one of those types: Assigner of Instant Nicknames.

"Bye"—Crusty Toad—"Henry."

My mom walks in the back door as they walk out the front. She's carrying two armloads of groceries. "Caymen, there are a few more bags; can you get them?" She heads straight for the stairs.

"You want me to leave the store?" It sounds like a lame question, but she's really particular about leaving the sales floor. First, because dolls are expensive and if any of them ever got stolen that would be a Big Deal. We don't have any type of video surveillance or alarm system on the store—too expensive to maintain. Second, my mom is huge about customer service. If someone walks in, I'm not supposed to let one second go by without a greeting.

"Yes. Please." She sounds out of breath. My mom, the queen of yoga, is out of breath? Was she running laps?

"Okay." I glance toward the front door to make sure no one is coming and then go out back and grab the rest of the groceries. When I take them upstairs I step over the bags she dropped off right inside the door and then set mine on the counter of our dollhouse-size

16

kitchen. That's really the theme of our lives. Dolls. We sell them. We live in their house . . . or at least the size equivalent: three tiny rooms, one bathroom, miniature kitchen. And I'm convinced the size is the main reason my mom and I are so close. I peer around the wall and see my mom sprawled out on the couch.

"You okay, Mom?"

She sits up but doesn't stand. "Just exhausted. Got up extra early this morning."

I begin to unload the groceries, putting the meat and frozen apple juice in the freezer. I once asked my mom if we could get bottled juice and she told me it was too expensive. I was six. That was the first time I realized we were poor. It definitely wasn't the last.

"Oh, sweetheart, don't worry about unloading. I'll do that in a minute. Will you head back to the store?"

"Sure." On my way out the door I move the bags she had abandoned on the floor to the counter as well, then leave. It takes my brain the whole trip down the stairs to remember that I saw my mom still in bed when I left for school this morning. How was that getting up "extra early"? I look over my shoulder, up the steep set of stairs, tempted to turn around and call her bluff. But I don't. I take my place behind the register, pull out my English reading assignment, and don't look up until the bell on the front door jingles.

CHAPTER 3

• • • • • • •

One of my favorite customers ever comes through the door. She's older but sharp and funny. Her hair is a deep red, sometimes bordering on purple, depending on how recently she had it dyed. And she always wears a scarf no matter how hot it is outside. The autumn weather occasionally justifies a scarf these days, and today's is bright orange with purple flowers.

"Caymen," she says with a smile.

"Hi, Mrs. Dalton."

"Is your mom in today, honey?"

"She's upstairs. Do you want me to get her or is there

something I can help you with?"

"I had a doll on special order and wondered if she arrived yet."

"Let me check." I pull out a binder from the drawer beneath the register that logs orders. I find Mrs. Dalton's name fairly easily because there are only a few entries, and most of them are hers. "It looks like it's scheduled to arrive tomorrow, but let me call on it for you so you don't come down here for nothing." I place a call and find out it will arrive after noon tomorrow.

"I'm sorry to bother you. Your mother did tell me that. I was just hoping." She smiles. "This one's for my granddaughter. Her birthday's in a few weeks."

"That's cool. I'm sure she'll love it. How old will the lucky little girl be?"

"Sixteen."

"Oh. The lucky . . . big girl." I don't know what else to say without sounding rude.

Mrs. Dalton laughs. "Don't worry, Caymen, I have other presents for her. This gift is more to humor her grandma. I've gotten her a doll every year since she turned one. It's hard for me to break a tradition no matter how old they get."

"My mother thanks you for that."

Mrs. Dalton laughs. She gets my jokes. Maybe because she's a little dry herself.

"She's the only girl so I spoil her rotten."

"What tradition do you have for the boys?"

"A kick in the pants."

"That's a great tradition. I think you should get them dolls for their birthdays, too. They probably feel left out."

She laughs. "I might have to try that." She sad-eyes the binder on the counter like she wishes the date would magically change and her doll would be here now. She opens her purse and starts digging through it. "How's Susan doing?"

I glance toward the back like my mom will come down the stairs at the mere mention of her name. "She's good."

She pulls out a little red book and starts flipping through it. "Tomorrow afternoon, you said?"

I nod.

"Oh no, that won't do. I have a hair appointment."

"That's okay. We'll hold it in the back until you come. You can get it Wednesday or really any day this week. Whatever works best."

She picks up the black pen on the counter and writes something in her book. "Maybe I'll send someone to get it for me. Would that work?"

"Of course."

"His name is Alex."

I write the name Alex next to the pickup line. "Sounds good."

She grabs my hand and squeezes it with both of hers. "You're such a good girl, Caymen. I'm glad you're here for your mom."

Sometimes I wonder just how much these ladies talk to my mom. What did they know about our history? Did they know about my father? As the spoiled kid of a wealthy family, he ran before my mom could finish saying, "I'm pregnant. What should we do?" His parents made her sign papers she didn't understand that virtually said she could never go after him for child support. They gave her hush money that eventually became the start-up funds for the doll store. And this is why I have absolutely no desire to meet my gem of a father. Not that he's tried.

Okay, so maybe I have a small desire. But after what he did to my mother it feels wrong.

I squeeze Mrs. Dalton's hand. "Oh, you know me, I'm competing for a Best Daughter in the Universe award. I hear this year it comes with a mug."

She smiles. "I think you already won it."

I roll my eyes. She pats my hand and then takes her time leaving the doll store, studying dolls as she goes.

I settle back onto the stool and read some more. When seven o'clock rolls around I glance at the stairs for what seems like the gazillionth time. My mom never came down. That's weird. She rarely makes me stay down here alone if she's actually here. After locking up, lowering the blinds, and turning out the lights, I grab the stack of mail and go upstairs.

The house smells amazing. Like sweet cooked carrots and mashed potatoes with gravy.

My mom is standing at the stove stirring gravy. Just as I'm about to greet her, she says, "I know. And that's the problem."

I realize she's on the phone, so I head to my bedroom to put my shoes away. Halfway down the hall I hear her say, "Oh please. They don't live here to mingle with normal society."

She must be talking to her best friend. She doesn't know I've overheard many conversations like this but I have. I kick off my shoes in my room and head back to the kitchen.

"Smells good, Mom," I say.

She jumps and then says, "Well, Caymen just walked in. I'd better go." She laughs at something her friend says. Her laugh is like a melodic song.

The kitchen doesn't like two people in it at once so it constantly shoves counter edges and drawer handles into my hips and lower back. I soon abandon the idea that we can both fit, and I step around the counter to the small dining area.

"Sorry I didn't join you downstairs," she says after hanging up the phone. "I thought I'd make us a hot dinner. It's been a while."

I sit down and flip through the mail I had brought up. "Is there an occasion?"

"Nope. Just for fun."

"Thanks, Mom." I hold up the electricity bill in a pink envelope. I have no idea why pink is chosen for lateness. Is it really the color that announces to the world (or at least the mail carrier): "These people are irresponsible failures?" I'd think puke yellow would do a better job at that announcement. "Forty-eight-hours notice."

"Ugh. Is that the only one?"

"Looks like it."

"Okay. I'll pay it online later. Just set it on the counter."

I don't even have to stand up to reach the counter. It's less than an arm's length away from the table. My mom carries over two plates of steaming food and sets one in front of me. We talk as we eat.

"Oh, Mom, I forgot to tell you about the guy who came into the store the other day."

"Oh yeah?"

"He beckoned me."

"I'm sure he was just trying to get your attention."

I keep going. "Also, nobody taught him how to smile,

and there was a lip curl at one point."

"Well, I hope you kept these thoughts to yourself." She takes a bite of her potatoes.

"No, I told him that you offered smiling lessons in the afternoon. I think he'll be in tomorrow."

Her eyes snap up, but she must realize I'm kidding because she lets out a sigh even though I see her trying to hide a smile.

"Mrs. Dalton was in again today."

For this news she offers a real smile. "She was in last week, too. She gets so excited when she's waiting for a doll."

"I know. It's cute." I clear my throat and fork a swirling pattern in my potatoes before looking at my mom.

"Thanks for running the store today. I got caught up in paperwork up here."

"It's okay."

"You know I appreciate you, right?"

I shrug. "It's no big deal."

"It is to me. I don't know what I'd do without you."

"I think you'd own lots of cats."

"Really? You think I'd be a cat lady?"

I nod slowly. "Yeah. That or nutcrackers."

"What? Nutcrackers? I don't even like nuts."

"You don't have to like nuts to own lots of wide-mouthed wooden dolls."

"So you think without you that I'd have a completely different personality and like cats and/or nutcrackers?"

Without me she'd have a completely different life. She'd have probably gone to college and got married, not been disowned by her parents. "Well, yeah. Hello. Without me in your life you'd have no humor or love. You'd be a sad, sad woman."

She laughs again. "So true." She places her fork on her plate and stands. "Are you done?"

"Yes."

She picks up my plate and puts it on top of hers but not before I notice that she hardly ate anything. At the sink she quickly rinses the plates.

"Mom, you cooked. I'll clean."

"Okay, thanks, sweetie. I think I'm going to go read in bed."

It takes me only about twenty minutes to clean up. On the way to my room I poke my head in my mom's room to say good night. An open book lies on her chest and she's fast asleep. She really was tired today. Maybe she had gotten up early, like she said, to work out or something then went back to sleep. I close her book, put it on her nightstand, and turn off her light.

CHAPTER 4

• • • • • • •

As I walk into the doll store the next day after school,
I'm surprised to see a man standing at the counter. He's
wearing dark clothes and has a dark, shortly trimmed
beard and a dark tan. Yes, there is definitely a dark theme
going on. He seems to exude it, and yet my mom's cheeks
are pink and she's smiling. When the bell on the door
rings, they both look over at me.

"Hi, Caymen," my mom says.

"Hi."

"Well, see you around, Susan," the strange man says.
My mom nods.

He leaves, and I say, "Who was that?" I tuck my backpack beneath the register. "Alex?"

"Who's Alex?"

"The guy who's supposed to pick up Mrs. Dalton's doll."

"Oh no, it was just a customer."

Right. I watch him walk by the front window. A single man in his forties is a customer. I almost say as much when she says, "I'm glad you're here. I have to run a couple things to the post office before one." She picks up two boxes and a stack of envelopes and heads toward the back door. "Oh, and Mrs. Dalton's doll is in the back."

"Okay, see you later."

The front door opens and I look up half expecting to see my mom's "customer" walk back in, but I'm greeted by a broody Henry. I don't know if he took a shower or if carrying a guitar case actually does make a guy appear more attractive than he is, but either way, it's suddenly a little more apparent what Skye sees in him.

"Hey, Caveman."

Ugh. He probably forgot my real name. "Hi, Toad. Skye's not here."

"I know. I was hoping I could play you a song I wrote for her. Let me know if you think she'll like it."

"Okay. Sure."

He sits on the floor and takes out his guitar. He leans against a lower cabinet, stretching out and crossing his legs in front of him. The dolls on the lit glass shelves above him and the wooden cradle next to him make this look like the setting for some trippy music video. He strums a few chords then clears his throat and sings.

The song is pretty good, bordering on cheesy. The line about how without Skye he would die makes me want to laugh, but I manage to hold it in. But by the end of the song I completely understand what Skye sees in him. I'm pretty sure I'm staring at him dreamily myself. So when the sound of someone clapping breaks the after-song silence, my cheeks go hot.

Xander is standing by the front door. He looks even richer today. The look consists of perfectly styled hair, designer clothes, and Gucci leather loafers with no socks.

"Great song," he says to Henry.

"Thanks." Then Henry looks at me for verification.

"Yeah, it was awesome."

He takes a breath of relief then puts his guitar away. I turn my attention to Xander.

"I've been sent on another errand," he says.

"Another day where mingling with commoners helps you appreciate your life more?" I could've sworn I said something equivalent last time, but the offended look that takes over his face lets me know I probably only thought it before. Oh well, it was a joke anyway (sort of). If he can't take a joke, that's on him.

"Something like that," he mumbles.

Henry stands up. "The Scottish doll is mine, so hands off."

Xander holds his hands up. "Not interested." I get the feeling Xander thinks Henry is talking about something other than a kilt-wearing doll. But since Xander is *not interested*, it doesn't matter anyway.

Henry heads for the door. "I'm going to sing the song in our set Friday night. Come. We're playing at Scream Shout. Ten o'clock." Scream Shout is a dive about five blocks away where local bands play to small, mostly wasted crowds for little or no money. I tag along with Skye occasionally, but it's not really my scene.

Xander watches him go and then turns back to me, all business. "My grandmother asked me to pick up a doll she ordered."

"Your grandmother?" I open the book, wondering if I had missed an order.

"Katherine Dalton."

"Mrs. Dalton is your grandma?"

"Why does that surprise you so much?"

I close my open mouth. *Because Mrs. Dalton is sweet and down-to-earth and amazing. . . . You take yourself too seriously, have perfectly manicured nails, and line your clothes with money* (or at least that's the excuse I give him for such good posture). "I just had no idea."

"So I guess she never talks about her brilliant grandson?"

"I just thought she was sending Alex in."

"I am Alex."

Oh. Duh. Xander. As in Alexander. "So do you go by Alex or Xander?"

He gets an arrogant smirk on his face like I had Googled him or something.

"Your credit card," I say, reminding him he had used it last time he was in.

"Oh. Yes, I go by Xander, but my grandparents call me Alex. I'm named after my grandpa so you know how that goes."

I have no idea how that goes. "Yeah, totally."

"So, Susan's daughter . . ." He leans his elbows on the counter, looks at a small wooden apple a customer gave us years ago, and starts spinning it like a top. "Do you have my doll?"

I laugh a little at how that sounds. "Yes, I do. Give me one minute." I retrieve the box from the back room and bring it to the counter. It surprises me that my mom hasn't opened it to inspect the doll. Sometimes they come cracked or broken, and the service we use is responsible for that. I grab a box cutter from a silver cup next to the register and cut the packing tape. "Just let me make sure she hasn't had any limbs amputated on her journey."

"Okay."

I remove the doll box from the shipping box, only displacing a few packing peanuts in the process, and carefully open it.

"'Mandy,'" he says, reading her name off the lid.

"Mandy's in good shape. Your grandma will be happy. I guess she's for your sister?"

"No. My cousin. Scarlett. That doll looks a lot like her. It's a little creepy."

"Your cousin wears lacy socks and knit dresses?"

"Well, no. But the hair . . . and my cousin definitely has that sly look in her eyes."

"So your cousin has a black bob and is looking for trouble?"

"Exactly."

I slide the box across the counter to him. "Tell your grandmother hi for me."

"And she'll know who 'me' is?"

"Doesn't everybody?"

"Everybody but me, it seems." He takes out his phone and pushes a few buttons.

"What are you doing?" I ask.

"I'm telling my grandma you say hi."

I roll my eyes. "That's cheating."

"I didn't realize we were playing a game." He offers me his first smile of the day, and I'm suddenly glad he keeps that thing put away. It's more disarming than any weapon. "Hi, Grammy. I got your doll. . . . Yes, a young lady at the store helped me with it. She told me to tell you hi. . . . No, not Susan."

I laugh out loud.

"Her daughter. Dark hair, green eyes."

I look down, surprised he knows the color of my eyes. His are brown with gold flecks. Not that I've noticed.

"Sixteen . . . ish?" He widens his eyes, asking if he guessed right. I shake my head no. "Seventeen?"

And a half.

"Caymen?" He raises his eyebrows at me. I shrug my shoulders. "Well, Caymen says hi. . . . Sweet? I don't know about sweet, but she's something." He's quiet for a while. "I *am* being nice. You should tell *her* to be nice. She wouldn't even tell me her name. . . . No, not because I'm being mean."

I love Mrs. Dalton.

I write down in the book the date and time the special order was picked up. Then for some reason I add the "ander" on the end of the "Alex" I had written before. I close the book and put it beneath the counter. He's still listening intently to something his grandma is saying. He meets my eyes at one point and then holds up a finger. He reaches into his pocket and pulls out his wallet and a credit card without even looking at it.

"She already paid," I whisper.

He nods and puts it away.

His grandma says something that makes him smile. The smile. What is it about that smile anyway? Maybe it's his perfectly straight and white teeth that make it so amazing. But it's more than that. It's a little crooked, one side going up more than the other. And once in a while his top teeth bite his bottom lip. It's a very unguarded smile, unlike the rest of his appearance, which is a fortress.

"Well, hey, Grammy, I gotta go. Caymen is staring at me, probably wondering if I'm ever going to leave her store so she can get back to work."

It's weird to hear him say my name. It makes him seem like more than just some random customer. Almost like we know each other now.

He pockets his phone. "Caymen."

"Xander."

"Does this mean I won the game?"

"I didn't realize we were playing a game."

He picks up the doll and backs away with his lower-lip-biting smile. "I think you did."

CHAPTER 5

• • • • • • •

About a year ago my mom started booking little girl
birthday parties in the back room of the store. It
sounded ridiculous at the time (still does), but she had
a vision of ordering unfinished dolls and then having
the girls come in and pick out the finishing touches—
clothes, hair color, eye color—so they could go home
with their own personalized doll. At first my mom let
them paint on the eyes, but that turned into Creep Show
101. So now I sit at the register painting eyes while my
mom stays with the party in the back and helps them
pick outfits and hair. On a good day we finish with a

hundred dollars in our pockets. On most Saturdays we're lucky to break even (my mom is a sucker and lets the kids pick more than the three allotted clothing items).

Today I think we made twenty bucks, and I'm wishing beyond anything that we would stop booking Saturday parties. But it makes my mom happy—some nonsense about the laughter of little children—so I don't complain. The girls giggle their way out of the store, clutching their newly clothed dolls and touching everything as they go. My mom will spend the next two hours cleaning up the "party room" (formerly known as the break room).

I look up when Skye walks in, Henry tagging along behind her. "We missed you last night," she says.

I search my memory but come up empty. "What was last night?"

"My band's show at Scream Shout," Henry says with a "duh" in his voice.

"Oh yeah. How'd it go?"

Skye smiles. "He wrote me a song."

Henry sets down his guitar and plops down next to it. "We thought we'd do a repeat of the night."

"Awesome," I say, looking over the list my mom made of the doll clothes we were running low on and checking off the ones I'd already ordered.

"She sounds like she's not excited, but she totally is,"

Skye says to Henry.

"Totally," I assure him dryly.

He strums a few chords. "Caveman has no life," he sings. I throw my pen at him, but then I need it back so I walk to where it landed on the floor behind him and pick it up.

Skye laughs. "She has a life, Henry. It's just a boring one."

"Considering I'm with you half the time, Skye, I'd watch what you say."

"Caveman has a boring life," he sings. "She needs some toil and strife."

"No, I'm fine with boringness, thank you." In fact I've settled into my monotonous life pretty well, only feeling the urge to rip my hair out about once a week now.

Skye straightens a doll on the shelf beside her. "But seriously, Caymen, you should've come last night. Why didn't you?"

"What time did you get home?" I ask.

"I don't know . . . two-ish."

"And that's why I didn't go. I had to work this morning."

"It's like she's a grown-up already," Henry says.

Who asked you?

"Play her a song, Henry. A real one."

"Okay."

As he starts to play Skye grabs the paper from my hands and puts it on the counter. "Just take a little break." She drags me to the floor in front of Henry. While he sings she looks over at me. "Oh, someone asked about you last night."

"Where?"

"At Scream Shout."

"Who?"

"I don't know, some kid who looked like he could've owned the place. Dressed like a fancy-pants. Super white teeth."

For some reason this news sends a jolt of fear through me. "Xander?"

She shrugs. "I don't know. He didn't say his name."

"What *did* he say?"

"Well, I overheard him talking to some guy behind me. He said, 'Do you know a girl named Caymen?' The guy said he didn't. When I turned around to tell him I knew you he was already walking away."

"And he left?"

"No, he stayed for a while, listened to Henry play, ordered a soda. Then he left."

Xander was looking for me. Not good. Mr. Rich and his completely over-the-top lifestyle need to stay away. "Was he alone?"

"No. Some girl was with him. She had short dark hair. Looked like she was bored."

His cousin maybe? I shrug.

"Who is he?"

"Just the grandson of some customer."

"The rich grandson of some rich customer?"

"Yeah."

"We should have more rich friends. It would take our entertainment to the next level."

"What are you talking about?" I point to Henry. "This is completely high-class. We have our own personal musician."

"You guys aren't even listening to my song," Henry complains.

"Sorry. It sounds great, babe."

He stops playing and returns his guitar to the case. "Caveman, I'm going to do you a favor."

"Please don't."

"Hear me out. I'm going to set you up with a friend. We can double." He looks at Skye. "Tic. He's the lead singer of Crusty Toads."

Skye gets a huge smile. "Oh yeah, he's so cool. You'll love him, Caymen."

"Tick? As in a blood-sucking insect?"

"No, as in a twitch. A tic." He blinks hard, imitating what I assume is a twitch. "It's not his real name."

"No kidding," I say.

"It's true. But I forgot his real name. Seriously, you guys would be perfect for each other. You'll like him."

I stand and grab my paper again. "No. I don't want to go out." And I definitely don't want to go on a blind date with someone named Tic who *Henry* thinks is perfect for me.

"Please, please, please," Skye begs, tugging on my arm.

"I don't even know the guy. I'll feel pathetic."

"We can change that. I'll send him in your store one day this week to say hi," Henry says.

I whirl on him. "Don't you dare."

"That sounds like a challenge," he says with a laugh.

"No, it's not, Toad. Don't do this." Would it be wrong if I sicced one of the dolls on him?

"Don't worry. I'll be sly about it. I won't tell him you want to go out with him or anything."

"Well, that's good considering I *don't* want to go out with him."

Skye sings the word "Anxiety."

Henry laughs again and stands up. "No worries, Caveman, you'll be okay. Just be yourself."

Not the "be yourself" line. I loathe that line. As if Myself and Tic have met before and gotten along, so all I have to do is make sure Myself is there this time. So illogical.

"You ready to go, Die?"

"Yeah. I'll see you soon." She smiles a really sneaky smile and I groan. This is so not cool. They are going to send some guy named Tic into my store and there is nothing I can do about it.

CHAPTER 6

●　　●　　●　　●　　●　　●　　●

After a week of anxiously looking up every time the bell on the door rings, I start to think maybe Skye had talked Henry out of the horrible threat of sending Tic into my store. But then it happens one Monday afternoon. A guy walks into the doll store holding a stack of papers.

He has short, curly black hair and mocha skin. A lip ring draws even more attention to his large lips. He's wearing jeans tucked into army boots and a T-shirt that says, *My band is cooler than your band*. In a tortured sort of way he's actually very attractive. And *way* too cool for me. I wonder why Skye's not dating *this* guy. He seems like a far better match for her.

"Hey," he says. His voice is raspy, like he just woke up or needs to clear his throat. "Henry told me you guys would be willing to put some flyers on your counter for our next show." He looks around.

"I'm sure the old ladies would love a rock concert," I say.

He lowers his brow. "Yeah, Henry seemed to think . . ." He trails off as he eyes a porcelain baby inside a bassinet. "Maybe I got the wrong store."

"No. It's fine. Just put them right here."

He walks over and sets a small stack on the counter then gives me a once-over. He must like what he sees because he says, "You should come," pointing to the flyer.

The flyer has a picture of a toad that looks like it just met the grill of a semitruck. Who designed that thing? Across its belly it says, "Crusty Toads." Then at the bottom it reads, "Friday night, ten o'clock, Scream Shout."

On the tip of my tongue something sarcastic about the flyers is ready to spew forth, but then I stop myself. "Yeah, I'll try."

"That sounds like what you really mean is that it's the last thing you want to do." He blinks hard, reminding me how he got his nickname. "I'm the singer. Does that make you want to go more or less?"

I smile. "Maybe a little more."

"I'm Mason." Much better than Tic.

"Caymen."

Please don't turn it into a nickname.

"Good to meet you, Caymen."

Five points.

"So what are the chances I'll actually see you Friday night?"

I look down at the flyer again then back up at him. "Pretty decent."

He tugs on his lip ring. "Tell the old ladies that it'll be rockin'."

"I will."

Just as he starts to leave my mom comes in the back door and he stops.

"Hi," she says.

"Mom, this is Mason. Mason, my mom, Susan."

"Hi, Susan, good to meet you."

"You, too." She points to the ceiling. "Caymen, I'll be upstairs making some phone calls if you need me." Her shoulders are slumped, and she reaches for the banister of the stairs.

"Everything okay?"

"Yeah . . . I . . . yes, I'm fine."

I watch her go then look back to Mason.

He taps the stack of flyers on the counter. "See you

Friday." He gives me a single wave as he walks out the door.

I bite my lip and stare at the toad on the paper. I need a new outfit or a new haircut. Something new. I make sure no one is coming through the front door then go into my mom's office to see if she's written my paycheck yet. She usually leaves it in an envelope in her desk. It's not much and I've told her a million times I feel weird about being paid, but she insists.

In the right-hand drawer is the balance book, bulging with receipts and loose papers. I pull it out and flip to the end where I've seen her pull my paycheck from several times. There's nothing there. I start to shut the book but a flash of red catches my eye. Scanning down the page, my eyes stop on the last number, a red "2,253.00." That's more than we spend in a month. I know. I do the bills sometimes.

My heart thumps out of control and guilt constricts my breathing. Here I was rooting around for my paycheck and my mom can't afford to pay me. We're beyond broke. No wonder my mom's seemed stressed recently. Does this mean we're going to lose the store? For just one second I think of a life without the doll store.

For that one second I feel free.

CHAPTER 7

• • • • • • •

I stare at the long mirror hanging in my room. Even when I back up as far as I can I can't see my entire body. My room is too small. I had straightened my hair, put on my best jeans and a black T-shirt, and laced up my purple boots. Nothing new. I wrestled with the fact that this wasn't a good idea at all. In eight hours from this minute I have to be awake and getting ready for work. Knowing how bad-off the store is makes me feel guilty. Like I haven't done enough. For the hundredth time I tell myself that I don't have to stay long. Just make my appearance and leave.

My mom walks by my room then backs up. "I thought you left already."

"No, and I don't have to leave if you need me."

"Caymen, I'm fine. Now get out of here. You look amazing."

As I walk the five blocks to Scream Shout, I take in my surroundings. Old Town looks like it belongs in a western movie. All the storefronts are made of vertical siding or red brick. Some stores even have saloon-style swinging doors. The sidewalks are cobblestone. The only things missing are the horizontal posts to tie off the horses in front of the stores. Instead there is a wide street and diagonal parking curbs. The ocean is several blocks away, but on a quiet night I can hear it and I can always smell it. I take a deep breath.

Two doors down from our doll store is a dance studio, and I'm surprised to see the lights all on this late at night. Wide-open windows on a dark night make everything inside as clear as on a movie screen. There is a girl inside, probably my age, dancing in front of a wall of mirrors. The graceful movements of her body prove she's been studying for years. I wonder why some people seem to be born knowing what they want to do with their lives and others—mostly me—have no idea. I sigh and continue my walk to the club.

Scream Shout is packed with locals tonight. I recognize

some people from school and nod hello. The stage can barely be called that. It's more like a rickety platform. Mismatched tables fill the area around it and a bar lines one wall. There are so many people I actually have to search out Skye.

"Hey," she says when I join her. Her hair is extra pink tonight, and I feel drab standing next to her.

"Hi. It's crowded tonight."

"I know. So cool. You must've made a good impression on Tic because he was just asking if I thought you'd show up." She nods her head to a door off the side of the stage where I assume the band is getting ready.

"Must we call him that?" I haven't decided what my impression of Mason is. But it must've been something or I wouldn't be standing here, giving up sleep.

"Yes, we must, Caveman."

"Please. Not you, too, Die."

She laughs. "I know, they're pretty awful, aren't they? It makes me laugh when you call Henry Toad, though."

"How's it going with Toad anyway?"

"Pretty good." Skye is extremely loyal. Henry would have to do something blatantly horrible for her to break up with him at this point. Not that he would. Aside from his heinous abuse of nicknames, Henry is decent.

I look back at the stage, waiting for its occupants. "I'm

guessing tonight you're going to be madly in love with him because he's about to go all rock star on you."

"For sure." She smiles. "And you are about to fall madly in love with Tic because his voice is like honey."

She's right. About the honey part at least. As he starts to sing I can't take my eyes off him. His voice has a soft, raspy quality to it that makes me want to sway with the beat. When I hear Skye giggling beside me I'm finally pulled from the trance.

"I told you," she says when I look at her.

"What? I was just listening. It's rude not to listen."

She laughs again.

When the last song is over Mason jumps off the stage and disappears into the back with the other guys. Henry comes out first, and he and Skye make out for a while right in front of me. Gross. Why do I suddenly wish I had someone to make out with? I'm good at being alone. I've pretty much mastered it. So what's changed? Xander's lip-biting smile flashes through my mind. No. I shake the image away.

Just when I'm sure that if I take a saliva sample from Skye's mouth it will come back with Henry's DNA, I say, "Okay, enough."

Skye pulls away laughing and Henry pretends like he just realized I was standing there. Right.

"S'up?" he says, then leans over to the bar and asks

for some ice water. He takes it and we search for a table. There are no open ones so we just stand in the corner talking.

Eventually Mason comes out and throws one arm around my neck. His T-shirt is sticky with sweat and almost reverses the effect his singing had on me. "Hey, Caymen, you came."

"Here I am."

"How'd we do tonight?"

"Really good."

"Did you bring any old ladies with you?" He looks around like this is a valid possibility.

"Almost, but she canceled on me last-minute. I guess some metal-head band was playing downtown tonight."

"Which band?" Henry asks, and Mason starts laughing.

"It was a joke, idiot," he says.

"Don't call me an idiot."

"Then don't act like one."

Henry pouts, and Skye says, "You're not an idiot, babe." Then they start making out again. Ugh. Seriously.

"Do you want something to drink?" Mason asks, leading me toward an abandoned table.

"Yes, please."

I sit down and he comes back with two bottles of beer.

He holds one out for me.

I put up my hands. "Oh, I don't drink. I'm seventeen."

"So? I'm nineteen."

"My mom says before I turn eighteen she still has the right to murder me." My mom always tells me to blame it on her if I am ever in an uncomfortable situation. It seems to work well.

He laughs. "Okay, that's cool." He sits down next to me.

I watch him drink for a minute then say, "I'm going to get some water."

"Oh." He jumps back up. "Sit. I'll get it."

I watch him walk away and can't decide if I'm feeling fluttery because I'm talking to the lead singer of a band or if it's Mason. When two other girls approach him at the bar and he turns to talk to them, I realize it's the first option. After all, I hardly know him. This makes me feel really shallow.

The bartender hands him my glass of ice water but Mason continues talking.

I stand, suddenly. I need to go. I have an early morning.

I walk to where we had left Skye and Henry and tap her on the shoulder. "Hey, I'm leaving."

She pulls away from Henry. "Wait." She looks around and spots Mason. "No, don't leave. He always gets bombarded by girls. It's not his fault."

"I'm not worried about him. That's not why I'm leaving." At least that's what I'm trying to convince myself. "I just have to work in the morning. I'll see you soon."

I walk away to say good-bye to Mason and hear her say, "Wait, we're walking you."

As we pass Mason I wave and mouth bye. But Skye says out loud, "We're walking Caymen home."

He gives me the wait motion with his hand and nods politely to the girl in front of him, finishing up whatever conversation they were having. He sets the ice water he'd ordered on the bar, then he's by my side. "I'm coming, too."

Henry and Skye walk in front of us, talking quietly. Mason drapes his arm around my shoulder. I'm learning quickly that he's a touchy kind of guy. We're silent for a block.

"I didn't realize you had to leave so early," he finally says.

"Yeah. I have work in the morning."

"We play again next week."

I'm not sure if he is inviting me or making small talk so I just nod.

"Thanks," I say when we get to the shop and I pull the keys out of my pocket.

He leans toward me, and because it never crosses

my mind that he would try to kiss me no matter how touchy-feely he is and with witnesses, I don't back up fast enough and am shocked when his lips meet mine. They're surprisingly soft. "Oh, uh . . . wow," I say, pulling back.

He doesn't back up and his eyes meet mine. "Thanks for coming tonight."

His smoky voice makes my heart patter to life and again I'm shocked at my reaction to him.

"Okay, see you."

Skye smiles at me like that was the most exciting occurrence ever. I just want to escape.

CHAPTER 8

• • • • • • •

The store doesn't open until nine, but like clockwork my eyes pop open at six Saturday morning. I try to go back to sleep but my body won't have it so I stare at the ceiling for a while thinking about the night before. What happened? Did Mason mean to kiss me? Had I turned toward him when he was going in for a hug or something? My brain feels the need to disassemble and then reconstruct the night in a way that makes sense.

It comes up with two logical possibilities. One, it was an accident and he was too nice to say so. Or two, he was really friendly and kissed everyone. Now that I have some reasonable explanations, I feel better. I just hope we don't run into each other for a while.

After an hour of unsuccessfully trying to go back to sleep, I roll out of bed and shower before my mom takes over the bathroom. I pull on a pair of jeans, a T-shirt, and slide my feet into fuzzy black slippers. With wet hair I go to grab a list of orders I had left downstairs the day before so I can enter it into the computer.

I cross-check it with the list my mom had made one more time. We still have an hour until opening so, with plenty of time to finish getting ready, I tuck the list into my pocket and head for the computer. Before I make it to the bottom step, I hear a knock on the front door. My hand immediately goes to my wet hair and my brain immediately thinks it's Mason. This scenario doesn't fall into either of the explanations my brain had come up with. Overly affectionate rock stars don't show up on the doorstep the morning after. We're not open yet so the blinds are still drawn over the glass. I don't have to open the door.

A second later the shop phone rings.

Mason doesn't have the shop phone number, does he? Would Skye have given it to him? I pick it up before my mom gets the chance to answer upstairs. "Hello, Dolls and More."

"A week ago someone warned me not to buy the

blueberry muffins at Eddie's, but I didn't listen and bought them anyway. Now at odd hours I get these insatiable cravings."

I'm so relieved at who's on the line that I let out a weird laugh/sigh combo then quickly clear my throat. "They're laced with addictive substances."

"I believe you now."

I smile.

"So are you going to let me in? It's kind of cold out here. I'll share."

My eyes dart to the door.

"I think this muffin might even have your name on it. . . . Oh no, sorry, that's my name."

"I . . ."

"You wouldn't want me to die of hypothermia, would you?" he says.

"I don't think it gets cold enough here for that." I shuffle on my slipper-clad feet to unlock the door then hold it open for Xander.

"Hi." His voice echoes in the phone I'm still holding to my ear. I push the Off button.

It's been so long I had almost forgotten how good-looking . . . and rich he is. But it clings to him along with the cold air as he walks inside. I relock the door and turn to face him. He's holding a brown Eddie's bakery bag and two Styrofoam cups with lids on them. "Hot chocolate." He lifts the cup in his right hand. "Or coffee." He lifts the one in his left. "I only took a tiny sip out of each so it doesn't matter to me."

Nice. Maybe Rich is a communicable disease. I point to his right hand. "Hot chocolate."

"I thought you might be a hot chocolate girl."

I take the hot chocolate from him and try not to register my shaking hand as I do so. That would imply his showing up out of the blue on my doorstep is tripping me out.

My gaze travels the length of him. It irritates me that this early in the morning Xander can look so . . . awake. If I saw him in the middle of the night with bedhead and sleepy eyes, would he still look so perfect?

"Your stare can make a guy insecure."

"I'm not staring. I'm observing."

"What's the difference?"

"The intent of observation is to gain data and form a theory or conclusion."

He tilts his head. "And what theory have you formed?"

That you're at least one step removed from normal. A chunky black ring on his pinky finger knocks against a rocking chair as he turns to glance around the dark store. I raise my eyebrows. *Maybe two steps.* "That you're a morning person."

He holds his arms out to the sides as if to say, *You caught me.* "I've made an observation as well."

"What's that?"

"You have very wet hair."

Oh. That's right. "Yeah, well, you gave me no warning. I don't wake up looking perfect." Like some people.

A realization comes over his face and I wait for him to express it. He looks over his shoulder toward the back. "Do you *live* here?"

"Yeah, there's an apartment upstairs." Now I'm confused. "So if you didn't know I lived here, why did you knock on the door before opening?"

"Because I assumed you had to come in early to get everything ready to open."

"This is where proper amounts of observation would've come in handy."

He laughs.

"You have no idea how many nightmares a porcelain-doll store can fuel. I have been murdered in a variety of ways by angelic-looking dolls over the years."

"That's really . . . morbid."

I laugh. "So what are you doing here?"

"I'm getting Eddie's. Isn't that obvious? And since you introduced me to the poison, I thought it only right that I share in the bounty."

"You like to look at the dolls, don't you? You miss them when you're away."

He offers one of his stingily given smiles. "Yes, I miss this place terribly when I'm away."

I set the phone on the counter, wrap both my hands

around the warm cup, and lead the way toward the stockroom. He follows. I sit down on the old couch and put my feet up on the coffee table.

He sets the Eddie's bag and his coffee on the table by my feet, takes off his jacket, and sits down next to me. "So, Caymen . . ."

"So, Xander . . ."

"Like the islands."

"What?"

"Your name. Caymen. Like the Cayman Islands. Is that your mom's favorite place to visit or something?"

"No, it's her third favorite place. I have an older brother named Paris and an older sister named Sydney."

"Wow." He opens the bag, takes out a muffin, and hands it to me. The top glistens with sprinkled sugar. "Really?"

I gently unwrap it. "No."

"Wait, so you don't have older siblings or those aren't their names?"

"I'm an only child." Mostly because I was born out of wedlock and have no contact with my father. Would that statement send him running? Probably. So why didn't I say it out loud?

"Note to self: Caymen is very good at sarcasm."

"If you're recording notes for an official record, I'd like the word 'very' stricken and replaced with 'exceptionally.'"

His eyes light up with a smile that doesn't quite reach

his lips, but that seems to imply he actually finds me amusing. My mother always told me guys were put off by my sarcasm.

"All right, your turn," he says.

"For what?"

"Ask me a question."

"Okay . . . um . . . Do you often force girls to invite you into their houses?"

"Never. They usually invite me in themselves."

"Of course they do."

He leans back and takes a bite of his muffin. "So, Ms. Observant, what was your first impression of me?"

"When you came into the store?"

"Yes."

That's easy. "Arrogant."

"Really? What made you think that?"

Does that surprise him? "I thought it was my turn to ask a question."

"What?"

"Isn't that how the game works? We each get a question?"

He looks at me expectantly. I realize I have no question. Or maybe I have too many. Like why is he really here? When will he realize I don't play with his crowd? What exactly made him interested in the first place? . . . If that's what this is. "Can I go finish getting ready?"

CHAPTER 9

• • • • • • •

"No. Okay, my turn. What made me come off as arro-gant?"

I stare at the crease on the sleeve of his T-shirt—a clear indication it had been ironed. Who irons T-shirts? "You beckoned me," I say, remembering that first day.

His brown eyes flash to mine. Even his eyes with their gold flecks remind me of his wealth. "I what?"

"You stay there. I'll be you." I walk to the far end of the stockroom and pretend to come in a door, holding a cell phone to my ear. I swagger a few steps, stop and stare at the wall, then hold up my hand and beckon him. I wait for him to laugh, but when I glance over he has a mortified look on his face.

"I may have exaggerated it just a bit," I say even though I didn't.

"That's how you saw me?"

I clear my throat and walk slowly back to the couch. "So are you the soccer player or the math genius?"

"Excuse me?"

"Your grandmother brags. I'm wondering which grandson you are."

"The one who hasn't done much of anything."

I toe the table leg with my slipper. "You do know who you're talking to?"

"I do. Caymen."

I roll my eyes. "I mean, I'm the queen of having done nothing, so I'm sure you've far outdone me."

"What haven't you done that you want to do?"

I shrug. "I don't know. I try not to think about it too much. I'm perfectly satisfied with my life. I think unhappiness comes from unfulfilled expectations."

"So the less you expect from life . . ."

"No. It's not like that. I just try to be happy and not wish I could do more." Well, I was getting better at that goal at least. And having people like him around only serves as a reminder of everything I don't have.

He finishes off his muffin then throws the wrapper in

the bag. "And does it work? Are you happy?"

"Mostly."

He raises his Styrofoam cup in a toast. "That's all that matters, then, isn't it?"

I nod and move my foot onto the coffee table. The order form in my pocket crinkles with the movement. I pull it out. "I should go. I have some work to do before we open."

"Right. Of course. I should go, too." He hesitates for a moment as if wanting to say something more.

I stand and he follows suit, picking up his jacket. I walk him to the front door and open it.

As he walks away I realize how little our question-and-answer session revealed about each other. I have no idea how old he is or where he goes to school or what he likes to do. Did we steer clear of those questions on purpose? Did we both ask ridiculous, meaningless questions because deep down we really don't want to know the other person?

He pushes a button on his keys and the fancy silver sports car in front of the shop beeps. That car alone answers any question I could possibly have about him. No need for any more. He opens the door and throws me *that* smile and I hear myself yell, "Are you a senior?"

He nods. "You?"

"Yeah." I hold up my drink. "Thanks for breakfast."

"No problem."

I shut the door and lean against it. Why?

It takes me several minutes to push myself away from the door and head upstairs. My mom's in the bathroom so I drag a chair to the old computer and start entering orders online.

"Did I hear the phone ring?" my mom asks when she comes into the dining area rubbing her wet hair with a towel.

"Yeah. I answered it."

"Who was it?"

"Just someone asking what time we opened." And that is the first time in my life I have lied to my mother. We tell each other everything. It surprises me. I should've said, "This kid named Xander—yes, he goes by Xander on purpose—who has his T-shirts ironed and wears jewelry." That would've been fun. My mom would've tried to pretend she was offended. We could've talked about how he probably gets his hair cut twice a month. She would've given a polite "it's best if we don't hang out with people like that" speech. I would've agreed. I do agree.

So what stopped me?

"Can you finish up this order, Mom? My hair is going to dry all funky if I don't get ahold of a blow-dryer."

"Yes, of course."

"Thanks."

I close myself in the bathroom and press my palms to my eyes. What stopped me?

Loyalty.

I didn't want my mom to have bad feelings toward him. Somehow the guy had managed to climb out of the box full of people I had already labeled off-limits with a permanent marker and he'd become different. And now, much to my irritation, I feel some form of loyalty to Xander Spence.

I had to change this immediately.

CHAPTER 10

• • • • • • •

Monday morning I wave good-bye to my mom and open the front door to the shop. As I walk toward school, I notice a sports car that looks just like Xander's parked a few doors down. I bend over to look inside, and when I straighten up again Xander is on my opposite side. I jump. He hands me a cup of hot chocolate and takes a sip from his cup.

I look at the cup—the same as yesterday's. "I only want this if you drank out of it first," I say, refusing to say, "What are you doing here?" That might give away that I care.

He grabs the cup from me, takes a drink then hands it back.

It surprises me so much that he acted on my sarcasm that I can't help but laugh. "I believe there's a meeting Thursday nights at Luigi's for those addicted to Eddie's muffins. If that doesn't work, I hear there's a pill you can take."

"I'm afraid my addiction is not one I'm willing to give up yet," he says.

I give him a sideways glance. We were still talking about muffins, right? "I'm sorry."

"So whose turn is it for a question?" he asks.

"Mine," I say, even though I really don't remember. But I'd rather ask than answer.

"Okay, what's it gonna be?"

"Do you have any brothers?" I know he doesn't have any sisters because his grandma said she has only one granddaughter and he already told me that is his cousin.

"Yes, I have two older brothers. Samuel is twenty-three, just graduated from law school."

"Which law school?"

"Harvard."

Of course.

"My other brother, Lucas, is twenty and away at college."

"Those are pretty normal names."

"Normal?"

"No Chets or Wellingtons or anything."

He raises one eyebrow. "Do you know any Wellingtons?"

"Of course not, but you probably do."

"No, actually I don't."

"Hmm," I say.

"Okay, my turn."

I smile but am nervous at the same time. I really wish I got to control all the questions asked. Then I could steer clear of the ones I don't want to answer.

"Are you wearing contacts?"

"What? That's your question?"

"Yes."

"No, I'm not. Why?"

"I've just never seen eyes as green as yours. I thought maybe they were colored contacts."

I turn my head so he doesn't see my smile and secretly curse him for making me feel special. "Are you?"

"Of course I'm not wearing contacts. You think I would purposefully make my eyes boring brown?"

"Those gold flecks make them look more amber." I want to kick myself for admitting I've noticed, especially when his smile widens.

"Well, this is me." I point to the old high school on my

right. It was built seventy-five years ago, and although its architecture is pretty and not seen much anymore, it could definitely use some upgrades.

He takes in my school. I shift uncomfortably, wondering what he thinks of it. Wondering why I care what he thinks of it. He probably goes to one of the two private schools in town. Yes, that is how many rich people live here—enough to require two private high schools in a small beach town.

His eyes are back on me. "See you later."

"Later as in you're going to be here at twelve o'clock to walk me home? Because I don't know if I can handle you twice a day."

He sighs heavily. "And my grandmother thinks you're sweet." Then his brow furrows a little. "Your school gets out at noon?"

"Well, not the whole school, but yes, I get out at noon."

"Why?"

"Um . . ." I gesture toward the shop. "Work release."

His eyes widen. "You miss half your school day to work in the shop?"

"It's not a big deal. . . . It was my idea. . . . It really doesn't bother me at all to help out." I know I'm rambling because deep down it does bother me—a lot—so I cut off my list of excuses and finish with "I better go."

"Okay. Bye, Caymen." He turns around and walks back toward his car without even a backward glance.

"Caymen," Mr. Brown says as I walk into science class a few minutes late.

"Sorry, I got caught in a thorny vine and had to untangle myself from its clutches." Which is actually sort of true.

"Although your excuses are by far the most creative, that's not why I addressed you."

The rest of the class had already started on a lab and I want to be doing it. It looks like there are actual chemicals involved.

Mr. Brown must've noted my gaze because he says, "It will only take a minute."

I reluctantly walk to his desk.

He slides several papers across to me. "This is that college I was telling you about. It specializes in math and science."

I grab the papers. "Oh yeah, thanks." I learned at the beginning of the year that it's better to just play along with teachers about college than to try to explain to them that you're not going for a while. I shove the papers in my backpack and take a seat at my station. At the beginning of the year we had an odd number of people in class. Mr. Brown asked for a volunteer to be alone. I raised my hand. I'd much rather do lab work alone so no one else can screw it up. It's so much easier not to have to depend on anyone else.

The next morning Xander's waiting outside the shop again, casually leaning against a light post, like we've been walking to school together our whole lives. He takes a sip of my hot chocolate then hands it to me as we start walking.

I take a drink. It scalds my throat going down. This isn't working. I need him to disappear so I can get back to my normal life of mocking people like him. So he can stop making me look forward to every morning. "So, Mr. Spence, your first brother is a lawyer; your second is going to some fancy college. What does your future hold?"

"I'm kind of like you."

"In what universe?"

He seems to think this is a joke and laughs. "I'm expected to take over the family business."

"What makes you think that's the same as me?"

"You work there, you live there, you help run the place. . . . I'm pretty sure your mom thinks of you as her eventual replacement."

I had resigned myself to the fact long ago, but hearing someone else acknowledge it triggers something in me.

"I'm not going to run the doll store forever."

"Then you better start sending different signals. Stat."

"It's more complicated than that." I can't just walk away and do something else. She depends on me.

"I completely understand."

Now it's my turn to laugh. He can't completely understand anything about my situation. It's more than obvious by his lifestyle that if he walks away from whatever his "family business" is it will survive. His family's bills will still get paid. He has a future of limitless possibilities.

"What will you do instead?" he asks.

"I don't know yet. I like science, I guess, but what am I supposed to do with that?" Knowing that would've required me growing up thinking I had a choice in the matter. "So why you?"

"Why me?"

"Yes, why are you expected to take over the business? Why not your brothers?"

"Because I haven't done anything. I haven't declared my strength. So my dad has declared it for me. He says I'm good in many areas so that must mean I'm supposed to be the face of the business. So they send me out into the world."

"What is the family business?"

He tilts his head like he's trying to decide if I'm serious. "The Road's End."

I try to make sense of that statement. "You own a hotel?"

"Something like that."

"What do you mean 'something like that'? You either do or you don't."

"There are five hundred of them."

"Okay."

"All together."

"Oh." Realization dawns. "You own all of them. . . ." Holy crap. This guy isn't just rich; he's RICH. My entire body tenses.

"Yes. And I'm getting groomed to take over one day. Just like you."

Just like me. "We're practically twins." By this time we're in front of my school. So is this why he started hanging out with me? I want to tell him that if he thinks he has found some sort of connection with me through our "similar" situations he should think again. But I can't bring myself to say it, and I'm not sure if it's to spare his feelings or mine. "I'll see you. . . ." This time I walk away first and don't look back.

CHAPTER 11

• • • • • • •

For the first time in as long as I can remember there are two customers in the store. As in two groups that didn't arrive together and both need assistance.

I'm not so good with kids—perhaps the real reason I'm banished to the "eye painting area" during parties. So without any kind of collaboration with me, my mom heads for the mom and little girl while I walk over to the middle-aged woman. "Hi. Can I help you find anything?"

"Yes. A few months ago I was in here—maybe it was more like six; I'm not even sure anymore—and there was this doll."

When she doesn't continue I say, "I'll have to look into that. We don't like dolls coming into the store."

She gives a halfhearted laugh. Maybe more of a nervous chuckle. "I know I'll have to be more specific." She walks along the back wall, intently looking at each and every one.

I trail after her. "If you can describe it, I can start a lineup of suspects."

"Dark curly hair, one dimple on her left cheek."

The woman is describing herself. A lot of people fall in love with dolls that look like them. So I study the woman a little closer and try to think of any dolls we might have that look like her. "Tina," I finally say. "Was she a sitting doll?"

"Yes." The woman gets a large smile. "Yes, I think her name was Tina."

"She should be out here. Let me look." I go to the corner of the store where Tina last was, but she isn't there. "Let me look in the back." We almost always order the same doll after it's proven itself a good seller.

The side wall in the stockroom is lined with shelves and those shelves house boxes big enough to hold a single doll. On the end of each box a name is written. It's like our very own porcelain-doll Crypt. About midway up I see the name Tina. I drag the ladder over and pull down her box, which feels very light.

On the floor, after digging through the packing peanuts, I find out why. There is no doll. Weird. I stand there confused for a moment, not sure what to do, before I go back out to the sales floor and interrupt my mother mid-sentence.

"Sorry, Mom, can I talk to you for a minute?"

She holds up a finger to me, and when she's finished talking to her customer, walks with me behind the register. "What's going on?"

"I just went to get Tina out of her box, only it seems Tina has been abducted."

"Oh yes, sorry. I sold her a while back. I must've forgotten to put her name placard in the drawer."

"Oh, okay. It just freaked me out. I'll tell the customer that we can order it for her." I start to walk away.

"Caymen," my mom says, keeping her voice low.

"Yeah?"

"Will you try to sell what we have on the floor before ordering another doll?"

I nod. Of course. That makes more sense than anything that had happened in the last five minutes. My mom wants to sell our inventory before we place more doll orders. It is a good idea to get us out of the hole. It actually eases my burden to know she has a plan for the big red number in her book.

"I'm sorry," I say to the lady. "Tina has found another

home, but I know we have some other dolls you'll love that look very similar to Tina. Let me show you my favorite." Favorite being a relative term, meaning I found her the least disturbing.

This woman was not biting. After showing her five dolls that look very much like Tina, she gets visibly upset. Her voice starts to wobble; her cheeks deepen a shade. "I just really want Tina. Is there a way I can order her? Do you have a catalog?"

My mom, having just said good-bye to her customers, joins us. "Is there anything I can help you with?"

"You had a doll in here that I want, but now she's gone."

"Tina," I remind my mom.

"Did Caymen show you some other dolls?"

"Yes, but those ones won't work."

"Is there something specific about Tina that makes her special to you?"

"Yes. My father bought me a doll when I was a girl. The doll was given away when I became a teenager and I have since lost my father. When I saw Tina a few months ago I couldn't get over how similar she was to my doll. I left without buying her that day but haven't been able to get her off my mind. I really just want that doll." A few tears escape the woman's eyes and she hastily wipes them away.

I look away, embarrassed for her. Or maybe it's more. Maybe I'm jealous someone can have that close of a relationship with her father that even after he is gone just the thought of him makes her emotional. When I think of my father I feel only emptiness.

My mom pats her arm and says, "I completely understand." But does she completely understand? My mother was disowned by her father. Is she thinking about that while comforting this lady? Does she think about that a lot? Or does she, like me, try to push it into the furthest parts of her mind and hope it never escapes, especially in front of others?

Mom continues. "I'm so sorry for your loss. Sometimes it's the little things that bring that special someone back to us in some small way." She waves her hand toward me and says, "Caymen can be a stickler sometimes, but we can definitely order that doll for you. We can probably even give you an extra special price."

I see how it is, make me the scapegoat. But I can handle taking the blame. It's the fact that my mom is once again not thinking about our financial problems that has me worried. Would this store have collapsed already if not for me keeping her from giving customers too many discounts, letting little girls pick too many clothes for their birthday dolls . . . ?

"For sure," I say. "Let me take you to the catalog so we can make sure we're all talking about the same doll here." I lead the way and then say, "We require payment up front before we can place the order." The last thing we need is to order a doll and have the lady never come get it.

My mom turns to me when the lady leaves. "Caymen."

"What?"

"I don't believe you were with that customer for a good half hour without finding out why she wanted that doll. We care about people, Caymen. I've been around too many people who only care about themselves to raise a daughter who doesn't think about others, even if they are strangers."

My mom's not so veiled put-down of my father was not lost on me, but her generalization bothered me. Wasn't it possible that money had nothing to do with the attitudes of the tiny slice of horrible rich people she had been exposed to? "You told me to try to get her to buy one we already had."

"Not at the expense of her feelings."

"Feelings don't cost anything. Dolls do."

She offers me a small smile and then runs a hand down my cheek. "Feelings, my dear daughter, you will perhaps learn one day, can be the most costly thing in the universe."

And that's the kind of attitude that is going to be the financial ruin of the store.

As I sit in my room later, her phrase plays over and over in my mind. *Feelings can be the most costly thing in the universe.* What does that mean? Well, I understand what it means, but what does it mean to her? Is she talking about my father? Hers?

I pull a notebook titled *Organ Donor* from the top shelf of my closet, flip to an empty page, and write the sentence my mom had said. This is where I keep all the information I have on my dad. I actually know a lot: his name, where he lives, even what he looks like. I'd looked him up on the internet out of curiosity. He works for some big law firm in New York. But knowing *about* someone doesn't equate to knowing them. So in this notebook I write all the things my mom has ever said about my dad. It isn't much. She had known my dad when she was young; it was a short relationship that ended fast. I often wonder if she really knew him at all. She could rarely answer any of my questions so I stopped asking. But every once in a while she says things in passing that I want to remember. Things that might help me discover . . . him? Me?

Even thinking that makes me angry. As if I need him to be a whole person. He left my mother to fend for herself. How could I want to be anything like him? But I'm practical, rational, and if I need to find him one day, I want to know as much as possible. I close the book and underline the title again. You never know when you might need a kidney or something one day. That is why I keep this notebook. It's the only reason.

CHAPTER 12

· · · · · · ·

The next morning my attitude hasn't improved much. Thinking about my dad always puts me in a bad mood. And the discovery of the empty doll casket in back made me realize the store is in even more trouble than I thought. I had been hoping that we always ran in the red; now I know we don't. But the fact that my mom ordered that lady her doll AT COST makes me realize something else: my mom might not have enough business sense to get us out of our financial trouble. Are we months away from homelessness? I sense the burden falling on my shoulders and I don't know what to do with the extra load.

I grab my backpack and walk out of the store. The air is cold today and bites my cheeks as I step outside. Halfway down the block Xander appears at my side and hands me my already-been-sipped-once drink. I savor the heat as it coats my mouth and throat. I can't believe we've been walking together all week. I hide my grin as I take another long sip.

"You okay?"

I look over at him and he's staring at me with a critical eye. "What? Yeah, of course."

"You just usually have something sarcastic to say right out of the gate."

Does he know me that well already? "Am I your required dose of daily abuse?"

"That works." He coughs a little. "Okay, new game. A challenge if you will."

"Listening."

"You don't know what you want to do with your life. I don't know what I want to do with mine. But we both know that we don't want to do dolls or hotels."

"That sounded bad, but I'm following."

"So I'm going to discover your destiny and you can discover mine."

"Uh, what?"

"I'm going to try to figure out what you like to do."

"How?"

"By trying different things, of course. Career days, if you will. I'll set up the first one. Tomorrow, one o'clock. Be ready."

"Tomorrow is Saturday. Don't you have a tennis match to watch or something?"

"What? No. I hate tennis."

I look around. "You might want to keep your voice down when you say stuff like that. You wouldn't want to be kicked out of the club."

"Are you trying to get out of the first career day?"

"I work Saturdays."

"Time to start sending different signals."

I picture our monthly calendar on the back counter. Remember filling it in with my mom at the beginning of the month like we always do. "We have a party booked. There's no way I can leave her alone." But maybe after the party . . .

He doesn't say a word, just gives me a raised eyebrow look. The pressure from the burden resting on my shoulders intensifies and anger surges through me. Why am I in charge of my mom's store? Why don't I have any choices about my future?

"Okay, one o'clock."

Saturday comes and I still haven't mentioned the outing to my mom. My short burst of anger had melted into guilt. My mom is stressed and the store is broke. This isn't the right time to rebel. Would there ever be a right time, though? One afternoon isn't going to equal the ruin of the store . . . at least I hope it won't.

The schedule confirms one birthday party from ten to noon. That should be perfect to help and then be done just in time to go with Xander. To go with Xander. On a date. Is that what this is? I try not to smile but my face seems to want to at this thought. I remind my face that Xander called it a career day and that seems to help.

My mom is in the back setting up the party while I'm watching the store. I know I need to talk to her, but I'm stalling. That guilt thing is gnawing at my gut. Nobody is in the store so I meander down the short hall and watch my mom set out little doll clothes on the table.

She turns to grab another stack and sees me. "Hey." She glances over my shoulder. "Did you need me?"

"No. I just wanted to make sure you didn't need my help." *You are a huge wimp, Caymen.*

"I'm good. Do you have all the paints ready out front for the eyes?"

"Yeah."

"Then I think we're set."

"Okay." I walk toward the front but force myself to go back. She's at her task again. I find it so much easier to talk to the back of her head. "Um . . . at one o'clock I'm going out with a friend if that's okay."

She straightens up and turns to face me, brushing off her hands. For seventeen years I've always waited until after the store closed to do anything. I've scheduled my life around store hours. All to avoid what I thought would be a look of disappointment if I asked. What I see makes me feel even guiltier: exhaustion. It's set in the crease between her eyes, the downward tilt of her chin. But not in her voice when she says, "Of course, Caymen. Have fun. What are you and Skye doing?"

"No, it's not Skye. It's . . . just a friend from school." I'm not quite ready to explain to my mom why I've decided to go against everything she stands for and everything I've always agreed with to hang out with King Rich himself. She doesn't need the added stress in her life right now. What's the point anyway when in a few weeks Xander will be done seeing how the other half lives? He'll get bored with me and move on, looking for his next taste of excitement.

She goes back to her task. "One o'clock."

CHAPTER 13

• • • • • • •

When the ten little girls come into the store, I direct them to the back and don't see my mom again until she starts bringing the dolls out and telling me the eye color attached to them. I focus all my energy on staying in the pre-etched lines of the dolls' eyes, adding green and black. Someone has asked for brown eyes so I apply a dark coat of brown. Then I squeeze a little gold onto the plastic tray and pick up the smallest paintbrush. Concentrating hard, I add little specks of gold on the brown.

The bell on the front door rings and I jump, sending a

gold streak across the black pupil. "Crap," I breathe out.

"I'm a little early," Xander says when I look up, surprised.

The clock on the register says twelve thirty. The party was supposed to be done a half hour ago. I hadn't realized it was so late. Had I noticed I would've gone to the back and hurried them along, like I have to do a lot.

He walks closer and rubs a finger across his cheek. "You have something on your face. Paint maybe?"

"Oh. Yeah." I wipe at my cheek.

"It's still there."

He's walking closer, and I realize I'm still holding the paintbrush with the gold paint and the doll with the gold-flecked eyes sits on the counter in front of me. "Will you watch the store for a minute?" I blurt out, jumping off the stool, grabbing the doll, and heading for the back without waiting for his answer.

"Mom, you've gone over."

"What? I have?" She claps her hands together. "Time to finish up, girls." She throws me a look over her shoulder—a combination of "I'm sorry" and "you know me." I do know her and that look makes me laugh.

"Are you done with that doll?" She picks up the electric heater off the counter to dry the eyes.

I look down at the doll in my hands. "Yes. Oh, wait. No. I messed up on it."

She studies the doll's eyes. "That's kind of pretty," she says. The gold streak across its pupil looks purposeful, like a shimmer. "I think you should leave it."

"Okay." I hand her the doll. "My friend is here." Her eyes fly around the room with the announcement. "I won't leave until the girls are gone, but just leave the mess for when I get back. I'll help you."

"Sounds good."

I head back out front. Behind me my mom says, "Okay, let's get this dolly's clothes on."

Xander is staring at a business card again when I come back out.

"There's no hidden message there," I say.

He puts the card back down. "You don't have a cell phone."

"Did the card tell you that?" I clean up the paints, closing their lids, and then wrap the paintbrushes in a paper towel to rinse off in the back. I glance over my shoulder, hoping my mom doesn't come out right now. I'm trying to figure out how to ask Xander to leave the store without making the reason obvious.

"You're never holding one, you don't have a square lump in the pocket of your jeans, and you haven't given me the number."

"Your observation skills are getting better. Although I don't think the last factor proves your theory." I put

the paints in a plastic bin. "I'll be right back again. Why
don't you wait for me in the car, okay?"

He doesn't move.

"I shouldn't be long. I'll be right there."

"Okay."

I wait for him to walk toward the door then take the
paintbrushes to the sink in the party room, rinse them
with soap and water, then put them in a jar to dry. The
girls are gathering up their things and comparing dolls.
I hurry ahead of the group and when I round the corner
see Xander still standing there. I stop in my tracks and
the kids push around me. He smiles as the girls sweep by
his legs. I whirl back around and maneuver through a
few girls, blocking my mom's view.

"What's wrong?" she asks.

"I think one of the kids left her jacket back there."

"Okay. I'll go grab it."

One little girl stops by Xander. "You look like my
Ken doll," she says, staring up at him.

"I do?" he says.

She nods.

"Do you know who you look like?" He squats
and starts to pull out his phone, but by this time I've
reached him. I grab hold of his arm and drag him out
the door.

"We have to go."

He lets out a grunt. "Caymen, I was talking to that little girl."

"Who is clearly delusional."

"Thanks a lot."

"Clearly you look more like Derek, the brunette, than Ken." I walk him all the way to his car and then say, "I'll be right back."

My mom has come out of the back room by the time I get inside. "I didn't see a jacket back there."

"I must've heard her wrong. Sorry."

"Okay." She sighs. "That was a fun party. The birthday girl couldn't stop hugging her doll."

"They seemed to have a good time." I shift nervously from one foot to another. "Anyway, my friend is waiting. I'll see you later?" I head quickly for the door.

"Hey, Picasso!" she calls.

I stop, thinking she's seen Xander outside and is going to call me out. I turn slowly.

"You have paint on your face." She sticks her thumb in her mouth then comes at me with it.

"Don't you dare." I wipe at my cheek.

She laughs. "Have fun."

"Thanks, Mom. I'm sorry to leave you by yourself."

"It's fine, Caymen."

"Thanks."

Xander is sitting in his car fiddling with the radio

when I get in. The smell of new leather assaults my senses. His car has more buttons and screens than I've ever seen in a car in my life.

He turns off the radio as I buckle my seat belt. "So you're saying even if you had a cell phone, you wouldn't give me the phone number?"

It takes me a second to realize he's picking up our previous conversation. "I didn't say that. I just said that wasn't a concrete factor to prove your theory."

He lowers the visor in front of me and flips open the mirror. "You still have paint on your face." He runs a finger down my cheek, tracing the paint line. My breath catches for a moment when his finger seems to linger a second longer than necessary.

"Stubborn paint." I turn my head to see the blue streak better. I rub it until it's gone.

Xander opens the compartment above my knees and takes out a pair of leather gloves. As he pulls them on, I can't help but laugh.

"What?"

"You have driving gloves."

"And?"

"And it's funny."

"Funny adorable?"

I shake my head. "If you say so."

He revs the engine a few times and then pulls onto the

road. "Why do I get the feeling you didn't want me to meet your mom back there?"

I thought it had escaped his notice. Apparently not. "Because I didn't."

"Well, that would explain the feeling."

"She's . . . Let's just say I need a little time before you two meet." Fifty years would probably do it.

"I'm sure I'd like her."

I laugh. "You would like her just fine."

He stops at an intersection and three women in brightly colored coats cross the street in front of us. "Wait, are you implying she wouldn't like me? I've never met a mom who didn't like me."

My gaze rests on his gloved hands. "There's a first time for everything." I watch storefronts go by for a while then ask, "Where are we going?"

"You'll see." Fifteen minutes later we pull up in front of The Road's End hotel.

CHAPTER 14

· · · · · · ·

"Your hotel? I'm pretty sure I don't want to be a maid when I grow up," I say to Xander as he drives through the parking lot.

"Even if you wanted to I don't think you could. That's a hard job."

I start to say something sarcastic back but am too surprised by his comment to think of anything. He parks the car in front and gets out. I follow him.

"This is not hotel-related. Except for the fact that the hotel serves as the backdrop."

"For REDRUM?" I ask in a croaky voice.

"What?"

"Haven't you ever seen *The Shining*?"

"No."

"Jack Nicholson? Slowly going crazy?"

"No."

"Probably a good idea since your family owns a bunch of hotels. I wouldn't recommend it. It's a horror movie that takes place in a hotel. So. Scary."

"What does red rum have to do with anything?"

"It's murder spelled backward." I finish with three warning beats: "Dum dum dum."

He gives me one of his are-you-for-real looks again. "Sounds terrifying."

"That's it. You have to watch the movie. I don't care if it makes it so you can never step foot in a hotel again. You're watching it."

He tosses his car keys to an attendant standing by the entrance and then opens the door. The lobby is gorgeous. Luxurious furniture, large plants, shiny tiles and . . . bigger than my entire apartment. The front desk people smile when we walk through. "Good afternoon, Mr. Spence."

He gives a small nod and directs me down the hall by placing a hand on my lower back. A chill goes through me. We come to a double-door gold elevator and he pushes the Up button, dropping his hand from my back.

There's an actual elevator guy inside wearing a blue jacket with big gold buttons. He says hi to Xander and me and I wave. He presses the button next to the number twenty. The elevator goes higher and higher until it finally stops with a ding.

The hall we step into is wide and leads to only one door. I have no idea what could be behind the door of what is obviously the penthouse suite that could possibly have anything to do with discovering what I want to do for a living.

Xander seems excited, though, as he turns the knob and opens the door. I'm overwhelmed by a lot of chaos and noise. Big shaded white lights are being assembled by a couple of guys. A few women arrange pillows on the couch. A man with a large camera hanging around his neck walks around analyzing different locations. Every once in a while he takes out a black stick thing and pushes a button.

"What are we doing here?" I ask Xander.

"It's a photo shoot. My dad wants some new pictures taken of the room for the site so he sent me here to oversee it." He walks to a large hutch against a wall, removes a camera from a case, and attaches a lens. "You are going to shadow the photographer. You'll be like his apprentice."

"Did you warn him that some girl who knows nothing

about photography is going to get in his way all day?"

"I did." He steps in front of me and slides the camera strap over my head then frees my hair from beneath it. I try not to sigh. He smells like expensive soap and laundry detergent. "He was flattered someone wanted to learn from him."

"If you say so."

His cell phone rings and he turns away to answer it. "What do you mean 'where am I?'" His voice has gone hard and cold. "Yes, I'm at the photo shoot. That's where you asked me to be. . . . Yes, well today I decided to . . . Okay . . . Yes . . . No, I have other plans tonight. Fine." He hangs up without saying bye.

I raise my eyebrows and look at his phone.

"My dad." He shrugs like his coldness on the phone was just an act.

"Mr. Spence," the photographer calls. "If you're ready we'll get started."

"Just let me change."

Change?

While he's gone the photographer calls me over and shows me a few basic functions of the camera and how and when to shoot. Xander comes back out wearing a suit that he totally rocks. A suit, coupled with his conservative haircut, makes him look a lot older than seventeen. He picks up a magazine off the table and sits on the couch. Seriously, I've never seen someone look so good in a suit. The photographer takes a few shots and then starts directing him. After he takes a dozen or so he turns to me. "Why don't you try a few while I set up the next scene?" And then he goes into the kitchen (the hotel room has a kitchen) and starts moving things around.

"You didn't tell me you were the model."

"Didn't I tell you my dad is making me the face of the business?" he says, and looks down. For the first time ever I see him blush. "It's embarrassing but he's found that people are more drawn to shots with life in them."

"So these will be on flyers and things?"

"Mostly on our website, but yes, flyers, too."

A website. Why didn't we have a website for the doll store? I smile and put the camera to my eye. "All right, hot stuff. Work it."

Looking at Xander through the lens of a camera is rewarding. I can do it without worrying about staring. As the day progresses I learn how to zoom in, focus on his smile or his eyes. His skin is amazing. His hair the perfect amount of shine and body. It's just a little wavy, which, although it's on the short side, makes it stand up perfectly.

I get to set up a few shots. I play with the light coming through the windows. First overexposing him, bathing his face in light. And then reversing the effect and back-lighting him so he is like a dark shadow, all edges and curves. I get a few with the ocean in the background. The hotel room has the perfect view.

"Loosen up, Xander," I say at one point.

"What? I'm loose."

"You're just so formal. You're supposed to be on vacation in these shots, right? Act like it."

"I'm in a suit. I'm probably actually at a business meeting or something."

"A business meeting for uptight employees?"

"Hey now." He laughs, and both the real photographer and I snap more pictures.

Just when I think the photographer has gotten all the pictures (and more) that he could possibly need, the hotel room door opens and a handsome middle-aged man walks in. I don't need Xander to curse under his breath to realize it's his father. The resemblance is obvious. They both have the brown eyes and the light brown hair, the high cheekbones and full lips. And they both carry themselves in exactly the same way: like they own the world. Xander's father scans the room and stops on me.

CHAPTER 15

• • • • • • •

Mr. Spence pauses on me for a full thirty seconds, taking me in from my six-month-old at-home haircut to my ratty Converse. Then he gives me a small nod of acknowledgment. I sense he thinks I'm an assistant to the photographer, and if Xander wants to play along with that, I don't blame him.

Xander looks between his father and me. If I was so hesitant to introduce Xander to my mom, I can only guess how he feels about introducing me to his father. I keep my mouth shut and maintain a tight grip on the camera.

Mr. Spence spots the open laptop in the corner. The photographer, most likely realizing what that means, says, "They are the raw, unedited shots, but you're welcome to look at the ones I've captured so far."

Xander stands. "But either way, we're done." He walks to the bedroom, and right before he gets to the door, he looks back at me and says, "Caymen," almost like he had expected me to know to follow him. I give him the *Are you sure?* look and he holds out his hand. My heart flips and I take a deep breath and walk toward him, but am not stupid enough to grab his hand when I reach him. I just walk past him and into the bedroom. He follows me in and shuts the door.

For some reason I'm out of breath.

The clothes he came here in are hung nicely over a chair in the corner and he walks over to them muttering something I can't understand. As he slides out of his suit coat and starts to unbutton the shirt underneath, something hits me. What if *I'm* his signal: another one of the messages to his dad to show that he doesn't want to be part of his father's world, a pawn in his game of rebellion? Is that why he started coming around? Hang out with the poor girl. That'll really get under his father's skin. I turn to face the wall while he changes.

I slip the camera off my neck and trace my finger over the silver button on top.

"Don't worry," he says, "I'm not changing in here. I'll go in the bathroom."

But when I turn back around, thinking I'm safe, his shirt is all the way unbuttoned. Regardless of the fact that his clothes are resting over his arm and he's heading for the attached bathroom, my face reddens at the sight of his bare, nicely defined chest.

Even after the bathroom door clicks shut, my heart continues to beat an accelerated rhythm. I walk slowly around the room, trying to calm it. Xander will not have this effect on me. I won't let him.

The furniture and bedding in the room are nicer than anything in my house. I let my hand trail over the rich material. When he comes out clothed I ask, "Xander, is this your camera or the photographer's?"

"It's mine."

"Do you think I can borrow it for a few days?"

"Of course. For what?"

"I have a porcelain doll fetish. Thought I could take some high-quality pictures of them."

He shakes his head. "And let's try that again. For what?"

"I kind of like the website idea. Maybe it's time our store has one." It could possibly save us from financial ruin.

"Hmm. That doesn't sound like the best way to show

your mom you have no interest in the store."

I shrug. "I'll just set it up and have her run it. Bring her into the modern world." Maybe a website could eventually take the place of me. People could place their own orders, we could make more money . . . then my mom could afford to hire a part-time employee. I try not to get my hopes up, because it could take months, but I like the idea.

He doesn't answer but takes the camera from me and nods his head toward the door, behind which his father exists. How bad is this going to look when we walk out there, Xander fully changed?

He must sense my hesitation because he says, "I don't care what he thinks, Caymen."

Of course he doesn't care what he thinks. He probably wants his dad to think something is going on between the two of us.

"Whatever." I open the door and try to walk out as casually as possible. My face doesn't get the memo and blushes. His dad is still studying the shots on the screen in the corner.

I turn back to Xander, wondering where to go. He's holding the camera up and fires off a shot. I put up my hand. "Don't."

"Come on, you have to be on the other end of the camera now. I have to see if modeling is something you'd want to do."

"Not even a possibility."

"With those eyes?" He shoots another picture. "It is definitely a possibility."

It may be my imagination, but he seems extra flirty. I swallow the lump in my throat. "These eyes are about to commit redrum."

He laughs louder than I've ever heard him laugh, confirming my suspicion that he's doing this all for his dad's benefit. "Come on, Caymen, loosen up," he says quoting me.

I cross my arms and glare at him. He takes one more shot with a laugh and then walks to the hutch, puts the camera in its case and then hands it to me. "Go crazy with your dolls."

"Thanks."

Xander's focus changes to something over my shoulder. When I turn around I'm surprised to see his dad behind me. "I thought you were here with the crew. I didn't realize you were one of my son's friends." He sticks out his hand. "I'm Blaine Spence."

I take his hand. "Caymen Meyers," I barely choke out. I'm still shocked he wanted to meet me at all. Did he want the camera back?

"Good to meet you," he says, seeming very sincere. Was he using reverse psychology on his son? Then he turns to Xander. "Alexander, a lot of those pictures are great."

Xander's face instantly hardens. "Good. So I'm done, then."

"I'd like you to work with the designer on a web layout and flyer."

"I don't have a lot of time for that, what with school and stuff, but maybe I can find some time in a few weeks." He puts a hand on my lower back as if trying to direct me out of the room fast, and I jump in surprise but then let him guide me toward the door.

"Nice to meet you," I call behind me.

"Alexander."

He stops. "Yeah?"

"Yes." Mr. Spence emphasizes the *s* on the word, and Xander's jaw tenses.

"Yes?" Xander emphasizes the *s* even more.

"Your mother's benefit is in four weeks. Your presence is required. And you will have the flyers ready for that night."

We step out into the hall, and Xander says, "I hope you're taking notes. I'm so much better at pissing off my family than you are."

"I'm taking notes." Find the last person on earth my mom (or in his case, dad) would want me to date and pretend to be dating him. Of course, my mom would actually have to know about it. But that's where we differ. I'm not using Xander. "Extensive notes. When my mom tells me to do something"—I point over my shoulder to the door we just exited—"I do it and pretend to be mad about it."

"So rude." He shoots me a half-smile, which I'm angry about because I thought that bit of sarcasm was at least worth a full smile.

He hits the Down button on the wall next to the elevator. "So, photography? Your future?"

"On the maybe list."

"I thought you might like it because you said you like science, which requires observing things and noticing detail. You're good at that and those traits serve well when looking through a viewfinder."

I look up at him in surprise.

"What?" he asks.

I realize I must be staring at him in shock and turn back to look at the blurry reflection of us in the gold elevator doors. "I . . . thanks . . . for noticing."

He shrugs. "I'm trying to find something you'll actually like. So you're up next."

"Yes, I am. And since we're all into this matching up the career day to our traits I guess I should find a career for you that involves ironing T-shirts or using lots of hair product."

He runs a hand through his hair. "I use very little hair product." We ride the elevator back down. "So next Saturday, same time?"

I try to mentally picture the calendar on the back counter of the store. I don't remember if there's a birth-day party written in. "Yeah . . . yes," I correct myself, giving him a smile to let him know I found his dad's correction irritating as well. "I think that'll work." We wait while the car is brought around. "Oh, and wear your crappiest clothes."

CHAPTER 16

• • • • • • •

I meet Xander on the curb Saturday, trying to avoid the same situation as last week. My mom seems to be buying the "kid from school" routine and until she forces me to introduce him I'm going to stick with it. He turns off the car and gets out before he realizes I'm standing there.

He's wearing nice jeans, an even nicer T-shirt, and some loafer-type shoes.

I point at his clothes. "Seriously? Didn't I say the crappiest clothes you have?"

He walks straight up to me. Normally he's a whole

head taller than me, but with him in the gutter and me still on the curb, my eyes are level with his chin.

"Hi to you, too."

I haven't seen him for a week. He was traveling for some sort of business stuff with his dad. For a minute I think he's going to hug me and my breath catches, but then he looks down at his outfit. "These *are* the crappiest clothes I have."

I give him a shove, satisfying the urge I had to touch him. "You're *full* of crap." But I know he's serious. "Okay, we'll have to make a pit stop on the way there."

We drive several blocks, and I point to the Salvation Army parking lot. "First stop, new outfit. Come. Let us reclothe you."

We step inside and the musty smell that only exists in the presence of old furniture greets me. It reminds me of Skye because we spend so much time in places like this. "Shoe size?" I ask.

"Twelve . . . Wait . . . we're getting shoes here? I don't know if I can wear shoes other people have worn."

"I think you just made a philosophical statement. Now suck it up, baby, because it's that or ruin your pretty shoes."

"I'm okay with ruining my shoes."

"Wait. Did I give you a choice? Never mind, you obviously can't be trusted with choices. We are buying your shoes here." I drag him to the shoe section. There are only three choices in his size. I pick him out the most hideous ones—high tops with neon laces. Then I put him to work trying on clothes.

While he's in the dressing room I look through the sweatshirt section. Flipping through the rack, I stop. In between an awful neon orange sweatshirt and a University blue one is a black dress. It has hand-sewn beading, a sweetheart neckline, and cap sleeves. I check the size. It would fit me. I bite my lip and look at the price tag: forty bucks. That's expensive for a thrift store. But it's priced right. The dress looks vintage. The best find I've ever come across. The fact that it's hidden between two sweat-shirts makes me know someone else has their eye on it, too, hiding it in hopes to come back later. But forty dollars is way beyond my price point. I still haven't been paid this month and I'm debating whether I'm going to cash my paycheck anyway. My mom can't afford to pay me. My piddly paycheck won't make much of a difference to my mom's debt, but it would make me feel a little better.

"I'm trying not to think about who wore these before," Xander yells from the dressing room.

"Do you need a tissue or are you going to stop crying? Come out here and let me see."

I move the next sweatshirt on the rack to cover the black dress. Even if I had forty bucks, where would I ever wear a dress like that anyway? To some fancy event with Xander? I hope I'm not turning into *that* girl, the one who daydreams about a guy she can never have.

The dressing room curtain slides open and Xander steps out while still buttoning the bottom few buttons of the flannel shirt. "I feel like a dork."

"It's good to feel like a dork once in a while. Now you just need a sweatshirt."

"I have my jacket."

"You mean your really expensive trench coat? Yeah, not going to work." I pull a gray one off a hanger next to me and throw it over two racks of clothes to him.

"Okay, I'm going to change back into my clothes now."

"No. You're wearing those out of here, boy. Come on, meet me at the register." I give the dress one last look and then walk away.

The lady at the register gives us the *Seriously?* look.

"Here," I say, turning Xander around. I pull the tag for the jeans off the back belt loop. Then I snag the one off the sleeve of the shirt and hand her the sweatshirt and shoes.

"That'll be fifteen dollars," she says.

Xander hands her a twenty. "Fifteen bucks? For all this?"

As we walk back to the car Xander is still surprised.

"I bought a pair of socks last week for thirty bucks."

"That's because you're an idiot."

"Thanks."

"Love your new shoes, by the way."

He rolls his eyes. "If humiliation is a career, I'm going to tell you right now that I don't think I'm interested."

"But you'd be so good at it."

We pull up to the cemetery and Xander looks at me. "What are we doing here?"

"Exploring our potential."

"Here?"

"Remember, I'm morbid. Let's go." I brought him here for a couple of different reasons. One, because it's free. I have no money to take him on the equivalent of some fancy photo shoot career day. And two, I honestly think Xander needs to get his hands dirty, relax a little. So far he's being a good sport, but he has no idea what I have in store for him.

"Hi, Mr. Lockwood," I say, walking up to the funeral home that's slightly elevated from the plots. Skye's dad is so cool. He looks like he should live in the middle of a graveyard with his long white hair and crooked hooked nose. I always wonder if he owns a cemetery because he looks that way or if he looks that way because he owns a cemetery.

"Hey, Caymen." He holds two shovels. "Are you sure you want to do this?"

"Yep." I grab the shovels.

"Okay, I got it started for you so that you could get a sense of the dimensions. It's past that oak tree down there." He pulls a walkie-talkie from his back pocket and hands it to me. "Let me know if you have any questions."

I hand Xander a shovel. "Okay."

"Gravedigger?" he asks as we walk toward the site. "Really? You thought this was a serious option?"

"It's not just grave digging, Xander. It's about this whole place. Living a quiet life surrounded by peaceful death."

"You *are* morbid."

Dirt clings to his hair and is smeared across his cheek. But even in his present state his confidence and stiff posture come through. "We're not going to be buried in here, right?"

"You caught me."

"You didn't think I'd do this, did you?"

Never in a million years. "I had my doubts."

"I wish I would've brought some gloves." He opens one of his hands and I catch the glimpse of a bloody blister on his palm.

I gasp. "Xander!"

"What?"

I grab his hand and study it closer, gingerly touching the broken skin. "You didn't tell me it was killing your hands." I had pulled my sweatshirt sleeves down over mine. His sweatshirt was a little on the small side.

"It's not too bad."

I unclip the walkie-talkie from the pocket of my jeans. "Mr. Lockwood, I think we're done."

"This hole isn't nearly deep enough," Xander says.

"I know. I just mean that *we're* done."

There's a burst of static on the walkie-talkie, then Mr. Lockwood says, "You ready for me to send the tractor?"

"Yes."

"Wait," Xander says. "A tractor is going to come dig the rest of this hole?"

"Yeah, they haven't hand dug graves in years. I just thought it would be fun."

"I'm going to kill you."

"This would be the perfect place."

He charges me, sweeping my legs out from beneath me with one of his feet but catching me then lowering me to the ground gently. I laugh as I struggle to get free. He pins my wrists above my head in one of his hands and uses his legs to pin mine. With his other hand he scoops up a handful of dirt and smashes it into my hair.

I laugh and continue to struggle but then realize he has

gone still. I suddenly become very aware of every place his body presses against mine. He meets my eyes and his grip on my wrists loosens. A sense of panic seizes my chest and I grab a handful of dirt from above my head and smash it against his cheek. He lets out a groan and rolls away from me, to his side, propping himself up with one elbow.

I lay there in the soft dirt for a while. It's cool against my neck. I can't decide if I just prevented something from happening or if it was all in my mind.

Xander lets out a large sigh. "I needed this after a week with my dad."

"Is he hard on you?"

"He's hard on everyone."

"I'm sorry."

"Don't be. I can handle him."

I've seen the way Xander "handles him." He shuts down, becomes hard, closed off. But if that's what gets him through, who am I to argue? I don't deal with my mom in the healthiest ways either.

My back aches and lying down feels great. I close my eyes. It's fairly peaceful, the silence seeming to press against me being surrounded by dirt walls like I am. Maybe here I can forget all the stress in my life. Forget that I'm a seventeen-year-old living a forty-year-old's life. Thinking about it makes it feel like someone dropped two tons of dirt on my chest that I wasn't expecting.

"What's wrong?"

I open my eyes to see Xander staring at me. "Nothing."

"It doesn't seem like nothing. You're off your game today."

"What game is that?"

"The one where you take every opportunity you can to make fun of me." He looks at his hand. "There were a million jokes you could've made about this." He shows me his blister again.

"I know. I really should've gone off on your soft, under-worked hands."

"Exactly." He brushes a piece of dirt off my cheek. "So what is it? What's wrong?"

"Sometimes I just feel older than I am, that's all."

"Me, too. But that's why we're doing this, right? To have fun. To stop worrying about what's expected of us and try to find out what we want for ourselves?"

I nod.

"My dad would die if he saw me here."

"We should've invited him, then, right?"

He laughs. "He wouldn't be caught dead out here."

"Well, actually, that's exactly when he'll be caught out here."

He laughs again. "You're different, Caymen."

"Different than what?"

"Than any other girl I've met."

Considering most of the girls he'd met probably had fifty times as much money as I did, that wasn't a hard feat to accomplish. Thinking about that makes my eyes sting.

"It's refreshing. You make me feel normal."

"Huh. I better work on that because you're far from normal."

He smiles and pushes my shoulder playfully. My heart slams into my ribs.

"Caymen."

I take another handful of dirt and smash it against his neck then try to make a quick escape. He grabs me from behind, and I see his hand, full of dirt, coming toward my face when the warning beeps of the tractor start up.

"Saved by the gravediggers," he says.

CHAPTER 17

• • • • • • •

Xander hops up and helps me to my feet. We throw our shovels out of the hole, then he gives me a boost out and hefts himself out after me.

As we walk back toward the funeral home, our shovels propped on Xander's shoulder, he says, "So this is where your best friend lives?"

I nod.

He laughs a little. "You live above a porcelain-doll store; your best friend lives in a cemetery. You've pretty much grown up surrounded by creepy things. Is there anything you're afraid of?"

You.

He meets my eyes, almost as if he had read my mind or maybe my thought is written all over my face.

I clear my throat. "Dogs."

"You've been bitten by a dog before?"

"No. But the thought of them biting me is enough."

"Interesting."

"Oh, please. Don't analyze the statement. Dogs have sharp teeth. They bite people."

He laughs.

"What about you? What's your biggest fear?"

He twirls a shovel on his shoulder once, thinking. Either he doesn't want to tell me or he doesn't have a strong fear of anything because it takes him a while to say, "Losing. Failure."

"Failing at what?"

"At anything. Sometimes it's hard for me to start something because I'd rather not try at all than fail at it."

"But nothing good ever happened without risk."

"I know this. And yet . . ."

We reach the back doors of the funeral home and he leans our shovels against the wall. I shake out my hair and he does the same. Then he turns me around and brushes off my back.

"And yet what?" I ask when I'm not sure if he's going to continue.

"And yet I can't get past it." His hands linger on my back and I close my eyes.

"Maybe you should let yourself fail at something. Fail hard. Then you won't be scared anymore."

"So should I go get the dogs now or later . . . ?"

"Okay, okay, I get it." He's right. I can't tell him to face his fear if I'm not willing to face mine. And I don't mean my fear of dogs.

"So are you just scared of the big dogs or do the little ones bother you, too?"

"You have dogs, don't you? The kind you carry in a purse?"

"No," he scoffs. "Of course I don't."

"Their size doesn't matter. In fact sometimes the little one are worse. They'll take off a finger."

"This coming from a girl who's never been bitten before."

"The thought, Xander. It's the thought."

He chuckles then pats my shoulders as if to say my back is now free of dirt. "Ready to go?"

"Yes. No, wait. Let me fix your hand real fast. Mr. Lockwood has supplies inside." I knock on the door then open it a crack. "Mr. Lockwood?" I step inside. "Follow me. If I remember right there's a first aid kit this way."

We walk down a long hall and I open the last door on the right. I stop cold when Mr. Lockwood looks up from a dead body lying flat on the table in front of him. "Sorry," I say. The man has a large cut down his chest with big staples holding it together. He had obviously had an autopsy performed. His face is sunken as well, not a fresh body but one a coroner probably had for several days.

"It's okay, come in."

The room is cold and a shiver goes through me. "I just needed a first aid kit. Some gauze and antiseptic maybe."

He points to the small bathroom attached to the room. "Right there." Mr. Lockwood applies some sort of foundation to the man's face.

It's hard to ignore the smell lingering in the room. It's not a horrible smell, but the smell of something being preserved. "Is he going to be open-casket?"

"Yes. Tomorrow." A large picture of the man when he was alive is taped to the wall next to Mr. Lockwood and he keeps referencing it.

"He needs some work," I say.

"We're getting there." He holds out a brush. "Do you want to apply some blush?"

"Xander, what do you say? Another facet to this career?" I turn around, but he is frozen in the doorway staring with a horrified expression at the guy on the table. His face looks almost as pale as the man who has his attention. "Maybe not."

I step in front of him and it takes a moment for him to meet my eyes.

"You okay?" I ask.

"Didn't expect that. I'm fine."

"You sure?"

"Yes."

"Okay, come here." I lead him to the bathroom and close the door, hoping that putting the body out of sight will help. I hold Xander's hand under some slow running water, gently rubbing it with soap. His eyes keep drifting to the shut door. "Stay," I say, searching the cupboards for the first aid kit. I find it and set it on the counter, opening it. Xander turns off the water and pats his hand dry.

I unscrew the lid off some antiseptic then take his hand back in mine and dab some onto the raw wound. "Does it hurt?"

"It's fine."

His breath touches my cheek with the answer and I realize how close we are. I wrap his hand with gauze and look up. "There, good as new."

The color in his face has changed to a sickly shade of gray. "Thanks," he mumbles, and rushes by me and out the door.

I thank Mr. Lockwood then leave. By the time I get outside, Xander is leaning one hand against the building and dry heaving into some bushes. This is a disaster. From blisters to puking my career day sucks.

"I'm sorry." I walk to his side and rub his shoulder. My mom always does that when I vomit. It doesn't help much but I like to know she's there.

"I'm okay. How much do you think Humiliation pays? Because I'm obviously really good at it."

"Never seen a dead body before, huh?"

"No . . ." He wipes his mouth on the sleeve of his sweatshirt and straightens up.

"Note to self: Xander has a sensitive stomach. Stay away from career fields involving anything gross."

At the car he pulls off the sweatshirt, nearly taking the shirt underneath with it and then steps out of his shoes. He throws them in the trunk, exchanging them for his nice ones. Trying not to let my gaze linger on the strip of still-exposed skin above his jeans, I tug off my sweatshirt as well.

"Do you want me to drive?" I ask, noting his still-too-pale face.

He hesitates for a moment.

"You don't trust me with your baby?"

"It's not that. . . . Okay, it's that."

"Rude."

He gets into the car.

I climb in the passenger seat. "You're really not going

to let me drive it? You let that valet guy drive it at the hotel."

"That was in a parking lot. And if you wrecked it we couldn't be friends anymore. Then where would you be?"

"Don't you have three others just like it?"

"Four, actually, but who's counting?"

I think he's kidding, but then again . . .

He starts the engine and pulls away from the curb. I look at the clock on Xander's dash. Five. It's hard to believe four hours had passed.

Xander moves into the right lane and starts to turn.

"Where are you going?"

"I thought we could get dinner. There's this French place over here that I love."

He's obviously feeling better. "I shouldn't. My mom's been stuck at the store all by herself half the day. I should get back and help her clean up."

"One more hour won't hurt."

"I should go back."

He continues his path down the wrong road. "Come on." He throws me his smile. I swear the thing could end wars.

"Okay. Then home."

"Of course."

●　●　●

It's not until I'm out of the car and walking up to the fancy French restaurant that I think about the layer of dirt coating my skin. Xander had smashed dirt into my hair and I can still feel some caked against my scalp. I self-consciously try to comb it out with my fingers. When we step inside, the people waiting in the lobby are all dressed up. I'm sure the hostess, who's dressed up herself, is about to turn us away. Xander has a streak of dried dirt across his forehead, after all.

But she offers Xander a gleaming white smile. "Mr. Spence. Your party is already here."

"Really?" He tilts his head at her. "Then lead the way."

"Did you have plans?" I ask as we walk behind her toward a back room.

"Apparently plans were made without me."

I have no idea what that means, but when we get to the back room a dozen well-dressed, perfectly put-together people laugh when they see him. One guy stands and then addresses the hostess, "See? Didn't we tell you we were with Xander Spence?"

"I shouldn't have doubted you," she says, then to Xander adds, "I'll make sure the waiter comes to take your order."

"Thank you." Xander steps into the room and walks around to an empty chair.

"You look like you've been doing community service," someone comments, pointing to his flannel shirt and dirty face.

Xander's confidence isn't shaken. His posture is still as straight as ever, his presence bigger than the room. There's a twinkle in his eye when he says, "So which fool is using my name to avoid waiting?"

The guy already standing, with glasses I'm pretty sure aren't prescription and a tan he probably pays for weekly, bows. "That would be me."

"I should've known."

"It's going on your tab, too," the guy adds.

Xander looks around and then spots me still by the entrance. "Everyone, this is my friend Caymen. Caymen, these are people you probably don't care to know but who I sometimes call my friends."

There are several shouts of disapproval followed by laughs.

I'm not sure I'm ready for this kind of initiation. I'm barely getting used to Xander. So when he pulls out the chair he's standing behind and gestures for me to sit, I want to go screaming out of the restaurant.

My stomach twists in tight knots over and over. It doesn't help that one of the girls on the end is glaring at me. Xander seems oblivious to the fact that I'm coated in mud and underdressed.

"Caymen. Come. Sit."

I clamp my teeth together because the phrase "Am I wearing a collar?" had been on its way out my mouth. I'm impressed I stopped it in time. I point back the way we came and mutter, "Bathroom," before I disappear without waiting for his response. Just when I'm almost out of hearing range, a voice says, "You taking in strays now, Xander?" followed by more laughter.

My jaw twitches as it tightens more. Why am I so angry? This only confirms everything I already know about the rich. Xander may be a slight exception, but those people in there are the rule. I change my direction and head to the hostess station instead.

"Can I borrow your phone?" I ask her when she turns my way.

"Of course."

I call Skye and she agrees to pick me up. Then I go back to face the room one last time. I watch Xander as I approach, before he notices me. He's listening to someone across the table. He has a small smile on his face, but it's nowhere close to bringing world peace. It almost looks like a practiced smile.

I tell myself to behave when I reach the private room. None of them acknowledge me so I don't feel any obligation to do different. I reach Xander and lean over. "I have to go. I'm not feeling so great." I feel slightly guilty for lying, but then I remember the "stray" comment his friend made and the feelings are gone.

He starts to stand. "I'll take you home."

"It's okay, I called Skye. I'll see you later."

"Caymen—"

"No, really. Stay. Have fun." I push on his shoulder, forcing him back down, then leave the room.

CHAPTER 18

I grab hold of the shop door and yank, but my arm jerks to a stop.

"Is it locked?" Skye asks.

For the first time I notice the windows are dark. I cup my hand over my eyes and press my nose to the window. My mom isn't there. Digging the keys out of my pocket, I unlock the door.

"Mom!"

No answer.

"Don't you normally close at seven on Saturdays?" Skye asks.

"Maybe it was slow."

Skye looks confused and she has every right to be. We've never closed early. She doesn't say anything about it but rounds a baby cradle and leans against the counter.

"I'll be right back." After looking in the party room and stockroom and not finding her, I go to the register and open the drawer. Empty. She must've taken the deposit. But why would she close early just to do that? I wasn't *that* late.

I rush upstairs and into the apartment.

"Mom!"

I'm greeted with silence. The answering machine we've had since I was a little girl doesn't have the red blinking light of a missed call. But on the counter right next to it is a note.

Caymen,
I had a 5:30 doctor's appointment. Since you weren't here, I decided to close the store and take the deposit on the way to my appointment. Don't worry about reopening. It's been slow anyway. Hope you had a fun day.

Mom

I reread the note. It's hard to tell from a piece of paper if someone was angry when they wrote it. I turn it over and run my hand along the back side to see how deeply the words are pressed into the page. Then I hold it up to the light to see if the handwriting looks rushed or angry. It seems to check out as being written by an average-tempered person. I sigh and place the note back on the counter then look around feeling a little lost.

I go back downstairs. Skye's on the phone so I grab the shelf cleaner from under the counter and start cleaning.

When Skye hangs up she says, "Henry is coming over."

The bell on the door dings.

"Like right now."

I let out a laugh. "That was fast."

Henry waves then looks up. "Why's it so dark in here?"

I point to the overhead lights. "The lights are off."

Skye laughs sweetly. "I'm sure he meant *why* are the lights off."

I'm distracted. "Oh. Right. We closed early. So what are you guys up to?" I look back and forth between Skye and Henry. They obviously had plans before I intercepted Skye for a ride.

"Henry came over so we could all hang out with you."

"Oh. Cool."

Henry flicks at his cheek twice, making a pinging noise. "Um . . . you also invited Tic over tonight. He'll be here in a little while."

"What?"

Again he pings his cheek. "We told Tic you invited him to come hang out at the shop."

"Wow, that was nice of me. Why would I do that?"

Skye smiles. "Because after he kissed you, you were smitten."

"Is that why I haven't talked to him in two weeks? Because I was smitten?"

She shrugs her shoulders.

"Tell me you didn't tell him that."

"Just relax. Come on, we'll chill in the back and then you won't feel like we're standing around waiting for him." She pulls me to the stockroom.

"So you *did* tell him that?" I sink onto the couch in the back room and think about damage control while Henry and Skye talk about some show the band is playing in a couple of weeks. Before I come up with any good plan, the bell on the front door rings and my heart stops.

"We're back here," Skye calls out.

What was I going to say? *Tic, hey. We kissed? What? Hmm, I don't remember that.*

I look up as footsteps shuffle into the room. "Xander!" Yes, I yelled his name but otherwise remained frozen. He had showered and was perfectly clean and back to his normal self. Looking at him like that makes me feel the layer of dirt on my exposed skin. I rub my arm. Why didn't I shower?

Xander nods to Skye and Henry then says, "Caymen, you forgot this in my car." He holds up my sweatshirt. "And I brought food since you didn't stay and eat."

That seems to be his theme: Showing up with food. Hot chocolate, muffins, and now French.

He sets it down on the coffee table and unloads several Styrofoam boxes. "Uh, I only brought two forks."

Skye crawls forward on her knees. "Who needs forks?" She scoops up a hunk of cheese-covered bread and pops it in her mouth. "Hey. I'm Skye. I saw you a couple weeks ago at the club."

Xander nods and takes Skye in, from the top of her bubblegum pink hair down to her unlaced army boots.

"Xander, this is my best friend, Skye, and her boyfriend, Henry."

"*Her* boyfriend," Xander says.

"Of course." I remember the day Xander had walked in the store when Henry was singing for me. He had gotten the impression that Henry was my boyfriend. Oops.

He shakes his head. "Good to meet you, Skye and Henry."

"You, too," Skye says, taking another bite. "Mmm, this is amazing."

Xander sits next to me on the couch and hands me a plastic fork. "Are you feeling better?"

"Better?" It takes me a second to remember the excuse I had used to leave the restaurant. "Oh. Yes. All better now."

He raises one eyebrow like he knew my secret. "So, Henry," Xander says. "Your band. Very impressive. Have you guys recorded anything?"

"No. We're working our way up. We have to earn money for studio time."

"I have access to a studio that you're welcome to use anytime for free."

"Are you yankin' me?"

"I don't . . . uh . . . yank. Call me sometime and we'll set it up."

Henry pulls out his phone, obviously ready to make sure he nails down the phone number before the offer is withdrawn. Xander relays the number.

"Where is everyone?" I hear Mason yell at the same time the bell rings.

CHAPTER 19

• • • • • • •

I widen my eyes at Skye and she bites her lip.

"Back here, Tic," Henry yells.

I stand, wondering if I should intercept him before he comes back, but it's too late. Mason in all his beautiful-hair-and-lips glory comes walking into the stockroom. He gives me a wide smile. "I thought you said you were coming last week. Instead you disappeared on me." He crosses the room in three steps and crushes me into a hug, smelling of cigarette butts and peppermint breath mints. "I didn't pin you as a girl who'd kiss and run." He says this next to my ear but I know everyone heard.

Then he kisses my cheek.

Talk about the king of bad timing. I pat his shoulder awkwardly then back out of his hug. A silence stretches across the room. I tentatively glance at Xander to see how he's taking all this. He has on his standard serious face.

"Dude," Henry says. "Xander just said we could use his studio to cut a few tracks."

Mason looks lost so I step aside and say, "Mason, this is Xander. Xander, Mason."

Xander extends his hand.

Mason gives him a sideways five. "Hey, man." Then proceeds to study Xander intently before adding, "I've seen you somewhere before."

"He was at one of our shows," Henry says.

"No. That's not it. Are you some sort of record producer?"

Xander gives a single laugh. "No. I'm Caymen's *friend.*" Did he emphasize the "friend" or was I hearing things?

Mason looks at me, his forehead still wrinkled as if trying to work out his thoughts. He blinks hard then says, "Nope. Have no idea. Thanks for the studio time."

"Sure."

Mason drops down next to Skye on the floor and lounges back on one elbow. With him on the floor and

Xander sitting stiffly on the couch, it's like an "Opposites Demonstration" is being acted out live for me. Two people couldn't be any more different than Xander and Mason. And the weird thing is that seeing Mason again makes me realize he probably is a good fit for me. Surely more than the rich guy I'm constantly assigning motives to for wanting to hang out with me. Is it sad that I don't even know my own type? Shouldn't I know my type? I slowly lower myself back onto the couch.

I don't know what to say to get rid of the awkward silence. Does Xander think I ditched him to hang out with another guy? I want to say I didn't know Mason was coming, but that would probably make him feel stupid. Instead I opt to say nothing and take another forkful of chicken as an excuse not to talk.

"Oh," Skye says. "Look at my weekly find." She thrusts her fist forward and the hanging chain of the bracelet on her wrist sways with the movement. "Ten dollars."

Everyone leans forward.

Mason runs a finger across a blue stone. "You wasted ten bucks on that? It doesn't look edible to me. We could've filled our fridge with that money. Right, Henry?"

"Amen, brother," Henry says. "I think we have a pack of mustard in there right now."

"Nope. I ate it yesterday," Mason says, and we laugh.

"You ate a pack of mustard?" Xander asks. "By itself?"

"I was hungry." We all laugh again.

"I once ate a bowl of mayonnaise when I was hungry," Henry says.

"Once my dad didn't shop for three weeks," Skye says, "and I ate some shriveled-up carrots from the bottom of the veggie drawer."

Mason kicks my foot. "You have dirt smeared across your forehead."

Xander laughs and I wipe at it. "Yeah, we were out at the graveyard today digging."

Skye lets out a little yelp. "Oh. I forgot you were doing that today. How'd it go?"

Xander clenches and unclenches his bandaged hand. "It was interesting."

Skye gives me a knowing smile.

Mason seems a bit confused but then asks me, "How's your mom doing?"

"She's good."

The room is completely silent for several beats until Xander's phone rings. I jump. He steps away from the group and answers it using the hard voice he seems to save just for his father.

"How do you know that guy?" Mason says.

"He's the grandson of a customer."

"A rich customer," Skye adds.

Mason moves to his knees. "What are we all eating? Foo-foo crap?"

"It's good," Skye says. "Rich-people food. You should try it."

Xander walks back over while hanging up the phone. "Caymen, I have to run."

"Okay."

"Good to meet everyone." When he's almost to the door, his gaze lingering on me, I realize I'm being rude and jump up to follow him. Once outside I stop in front of his car.

"You have some interesting friends," he says. The practiced smile from back at the restaurant is on his face and I don't like it.

"Yeah, they're fun." I point to his pocket. "Who was on the phone?"

"My dad. Hotel emergency."

"What does a hotel emergency consist of?"

"This time some idiot burned a hole in a customer's dress shirt while ironing it. My order is to find a replacement shirt, hopefully in town." He's taken on his business voice: serious and matter-of-fact like he's talking to a colleague and not me.

"Hopefully in town?"

"Well, it depends on the brand. We might not have

the retailer in this sprawling metropolis of ours. If we don't, I'll have to head up to San Fran or somewhere. I'll call around first."

"So why are you guys responsible for some idiot getting a hole burned in his shirt?"

His hand is in his pocket and he's bouncing his keys up and down. Is he hinting that he wants to leave? "Because the idiot that did the burning is one of our employees. Well, was. I'm sure he's been fired."

"Fired?"

It takes Xander a moment to register why that would shock me. "He just cost the company an important customer."

The wind has blown a strand of hair across my face, and when Xander reaches out to brush it away, I move it myself and take a few steps back. "Have fun with your emergency."

He looks down at the new space I created between us then shakes his head and says in a hard voice, "He's met your mom?"

"What? Who?"

"Lip-ring guy."

"Mason. Yeah, he has." Just once, in passing, but right now I don't care if Xander thinks more. I'm irritated. I thought Xander was different but tonight has proved to me that he isn't. I wanted him to be different.

"Your mom approves of him and you're worried she wouldn't approve of me?"

"Mason's friends have never called me a stray. So is that so hard to believe?"

"What?"

"I heard what your friend called me."

He gives a single, bitter laugh. "That's why you left? You should've eavesdropped a little longer because he was referring to my shirt. He calls flannel the 'dog-catcher fabric.'"

My chest tightens and I think about saying sorry, but that's not the only thing that bothered me tonight. "Well, thank goodness you'll never have to wear it again."

He pulls his keys out of his pocket. "Bye, Caymen."

"Bye." I don't look back over my shoulder even though I want to so badly. I want him to stop me from walking away. And I'm angry with myself for wanting that.

He doesn't stop me.

Back in the stockroom Henry is packing away his guitar and Skye is wrapping a scarf around her neck.

I don't want to be left alone. My stomach hurts. "Where is everyone going?"

"Henry doesn't like the offerings." Skye points to the food on the table. "We're loading up on some real food at the corner mart."

"Real food as in nachos and day-old corn dogs?"

"Exactly," Henry says.

I carefully add three seconds' worth of Mountain Dew to my cup then move to the Powerade.

"What's she doing?" I hear Mason ask.

Skye laughs. "It's her special mixture. She spent all last summer on this experiment. She has now discovered the perfect formula of soda fountain mixture."

"I'll have to try it," Mason says, the owner of the gas station trailing behind him as he walks. The owner doesn't trust teenagers and he always follows us around telling us the "deals of the day" in a veiled attempt to make it seem like he's not watching us. Right now he is telling Mason about the sale on beef jerky and Mason is messing with him by asking if he can mix and match different items. The only one amused by this is me. Skye is pumping mustard onto an oversized hot dog.

I finish up my last add-in and take a sip. Perfect. Skye may make fun of me but this was an experiment worth the effort. "How much would you pay for a shirt?" I ask suddenly, thinking of the hundreds of dollars Xander was about to spend on a replacement shirt for his "important customer."

"I got this one for fifty cents at the Salvation Army," Mason announces proudly, pointing with a stick of beef jerky to the band logo on his T-shirt. The owner intently follows the movement of the jerky with his eyes as if Mason is going to slip it up his sleeve.

"That's awesome even for a thrift store," Skye says with a nod, clearly impressed.

"Five bucks for these jeans," Henry says. "I would've been willing to pay six though." He lifts his shirt to show us a full view of his butt.

I laugh. Including the overly suspicious gas station owner, these are my kind of people.

Mason points and blinks at the same time, giving a loud "Aha!" that makes me jump.

"What?" I ask.

"That's where I recognize him from."

I turn slowly, following his finger to a *Starz* magazine on a rack behind me. In the corner on the front page is a picture of Xander.

CHAPTER 20

• • • • • • •

I probably shouldn't have bought the magazine. I'm already irritated enough at Xander. But I did and now I sit alone on the couch in my living room, waiting for my mom to get home, and read the lame article again. All it says is that "The Prince of Hotels" was spotted in New York last week to oversee the reopening of one of the family's hotels.

No wonder why he was confused I didn't know what his family's business was when we first met. He probably thought I was pretending not to know who he was. I blame it on our lack of cable. I may not have known exactly who he was, but I always knew he was a some-body. An article reminding me of the fact doesn't change anything. I crumble up the thin magazine and throw it at the glowing television. Two seconds later my mom walks in the front door.

"Hi," she says when she sees me on the couch.

"That appointment took forever." It would be really obvious if I pick up the magazine so I leave it there and hope she doesn't notice.

"Sorry. I ran some errands when I was done."

I point over my shoulder. "I made you a sandwich. It's in the fridge."

The lighting changes as my show goes to a commercial, and I notice my mom's eyes are red. I sit up and turn toward her. "Are you okay?"

"Of course. Just tired." She disappears as she walks into the kitchen that is separated from where I sit by a single wall.

"Really?"

"Yes. I'm fine."

I grab the magazine and shove it in my pocket.

After banging around in the kitchen for a while, she yells out, "Did you have fun?"

I walk the four and a half steps to the television and turn it off then wait for her to join me on the couch. "Yes. We went to Skye's and did some grave digging.

It was pretty cool."

"That sounds great. I wish you would've had your friend come in. I wanted to meet him."

No, you didn't. You would've hated to meet him. "He has a doll phobia. Some childhood trauma."

"Really?"

"Not really, Mom."

"You are hilarious, Caymen."

"You're getting good at sarcasm."

She laughs. "So is this friend a boyfriend?"

"We're just friends." But are we even that now?

"Well, if that's all you're looking for then you better watch it because you know the difference between a 'boy friend' and a 'boyfriend.'"

I roll my eyes with a smile. "Yeah, yeah."

"Just a little space," she says. "Don't go breaking hearts."

"You're like Socrates or something, Mom."

"I am, aren't I?" I hear a cupboard open and shut and prepare for her to join me on the couch when she says, "Thanks for the sandwich, sweetie. I'll eat it tomorrow. I ate while I was out."

"Okay."

"I'm sorry to come in and then crash on you, but I'm heading to bed."

"At eight o'clock?"

"It's been a long day between manning the shop and running around town."

I jump up and follow her down the hall. "Wait."

She turns to face me. The hall light is off and we stand in shadows. "Yes?"

"Please talk to me. Something's wrong." My mom and I used to tell each other everything. The distance I feel between us is my fault, I know, because of all the secrets we're keeping, but I need her to talk to me.

She looks at her hands and her shoulders rise and fall. She doesn't meet my eyes when she says, "It's nothing. Really."

"Please, Mom. I know what nothing looks like and it's not this."

"I tried to secure a loan today. I was denied."

I don't need to ask but I do anyway. "A loan for what?"

She finally looks up. Her eyes are bloodshot. "To pay some bills I've gotten behind on." She takes my hand. "But I don't want you to worry about it. We'll be fine. We're behind is all. We've been behind before. Let's hope for a few good months. We'll just have to be more careful."

"More careful?" How could we be more careful? We already spend next to nothing.

"Don't worry, okay? It's fine."

I nod and she gives me a hug. It doesn't stop me from worrying.

When she's in her room I shut my bedroom door with a horrible pressure in my chest. The magazine digs into my thigh so I yank it out of my pocket and smooth it flat. "Are you even worth all this trouble, Xander?" I say to his wrinkled face.

Monday morning I take my time getting ready. I've been trying to figure out all weekend what to say to Xander. I'm tired of the feeling that's settled onto my chest and threatened to stay.

When I go downstairs my mom is zipping up the green bank-deposit bag and tucking it into her purse.

"I thought you took the deposit Saturday night."

She jumps. "You scared me." She looks me up and down. "Wow, you look nice today. I haven't seen you wear that sweater in forever. It makes your eyes stand out. Is this for the special boy at school?"

If I didn't love my mom so much I would strangle her. "No, Mom, I told you we're just friends." And he doesn't go to my school. And . . . wait, was she trying to change the subject? It almost worked. "So what's going on with the deposit?"

"I didn't take it Saturday."

She didn't take the deposit? My mom is anal about

making the deposit. And didn't she just say last night that we are behind?

She must've noted my look because she says, "It's not a big deal. I'll take it over right when they open."

"Okay." I grab my backpack, smooth down my sweater, and face the door. My heart gives a little unexpected flutter, the first one since fighting with Xander. I smile and step out into the cold.

Xander's not there.

My walk to school feels twice as long as normal. Maybe because I keep looking over my shoulder or maybe because I've slowed down to give him time to arrive. He never does.

After school, while my mom is upstairs placing orders on the computer, I get out Xander's camera that I keep stashed in the stockroom desk and take more pictures of the dolls. I've never felt more motivated to get the website up and running. We could obviously use the increase in traffic. As I stare at the lifeless eyes of Aislyn through the viewfinder, a thought comes back to me: my mom standing by the register that morning holding the bank-deposit bag and how she tried to avoid my questions about it.

I strap the camera around my neck and sneak into her office. The first thing I look for is the balance book. The red number is even bigger, over three thousand dollars. It shouldn't surprise me; she had said as much. But it makes me worry even more. I open the side drawer where she keeps the bank bag and pull it out. It's zipped shut and I stare at it for a moment, feeling the weight in my hands, not wanting to open it and find out if the money is still inside. I have no idea what it will mean if the money is still inside. That she's still hiding things from me? Fast and painless. I slide it open and look in. Empty. Even though the money is gone, proving she made the deposit, I feel uneasy.

The bell on the front door rings, and I shove the bag back in the drawer and rush back out front.

A tall man with dark hair and a dark beard stands just inside the door. It takes me a second to place him, but then I remember he had been in the store a few weeks ago, talking to my mom.

"Is Susan in?" he asks, his eyes lingering on the camera around my neck.

"No, she's not." I could probably tell him she's just upstairs, but the feeling of uneasiness I felt in my mom's office has grown.

"Will you tell her Matthew dropped by?"

"Is there something I can help you with?"

His eyes twinkle and his mouth twitches into a smile. "No." With that he backs out the door. He walks by the front window, and I wait for a few seconds then quickly step outside, staying close to the building so he won't see me. He gets into a navy blue SUV parked a few stores away. I quickly snap off a few pictures, zooming in on the license plate and then up to his face. My heart nearly stops when his eyes meet the camera lens. The metal door handle digs into my back with my hasty retreat. He probably didn't see me. I had zoomed in quite a bit.

Inside I pick up the phone. Just as I'm about to push the intercom button, I stop myself. I don't want to tell my mom about Matthew over the phone. I don't want to tell her about Matthew at all. It's not that my mom has never dated anyone. She has . . . on occasion. But she always tells me about it. So I have to assume that who-ever Matthew is, he's not someone she's dating. And if she's not dating him, then who is he?

CHAPTER 21

•　　•　　•　　•　　•　　•　　•

Two days later I stare at Xander's camera bag on my bed. I had uploaded the pictures onto the computer and started working on the website. Anything to keep my mind off the fact that I haven't seen Xander since Saturday night. I go over the night in my head. Him bringing over the French food, Mason showing up, me stepping back when Xander tried to touch my hair, our fight. I had been giving him the back-off signals all along, but apparently he didn't take them until now.

I nudge the bag with my toe and sigh. For two days I had been contemplating whether to use the camera as an excuse to see him again. The whole "I just wanted to return your camera" bit. There are two problems with this. One, I have no idea where he lives. Two, I don't have his phone number. There are also two solutions to this problem. One, I could call Mrs. Dalton and ask for Xander's number. Two, I can show up at The Road's End hotel and hope to run into him.

Solution number two wins. My mind spins this crazy idea that if I show up at the hotel he will just magically be there. I can say, "I was in the neighborhood," and it won't look so obvious or seem too creepy.

Things never work how I imagine them, though, so as I stand at the check-in counter in the fancy lobby of the hotel, talking to the clerk, I resign myself to the fact that this is not happening.

"I have his camera," I say again.

"And like I told you before, if you leave it with me I'll make sure he gets it."

"If you can just tell me when he'll be in or give me his address or something, I can drop it off."

The look she gives me sends a pain through my heart. The look says, *Do you know how many girls have tried to get Xander's information?* I take a step back from the look.

"You don't want to leave it?"

I try to give her the look that lets her know I don't trust her as I say, "It's an expensive camera." My look doesn't seem to affect her as much as hers did me. The truth is if I were in her shoes, staring at me, I wouldn't give me Xander's info either.

I turn around and walk back the way I came, still clutching Xander's camera. So on to option one, then. I'll call Mrs. Dalton and get Xander's number. I need to return his camera, after all. It's really important.

The bag's strap is tight around my hand because I have looped it several times to keep it from dragging on the ground. My fingers are turning more and more white the longer the circulation is cut off. Just as I reach the door I stop. Why am I doing this to myself? Why am I hanging onto this so tight? To him so tight? It shouldn't be this hard. If it were right I wouldn't be lying to my mother about it. I wouldn't feel guilty about it. If it were right it would be easier.

I make my walk of shame back to the check-in desk and put the camera on top. "Yes. Will you give this to him?"

She nods and looks like she's going to say something— thank you, maybe?—but then the phone rings and she picks it up and I'm forgotten. I take a deep breath and walk away. I can leave him behind, too. Here, where he belongs.

As I drive home I notice kids in costume fill the neigh- borhoods. How did I forget it's Halloween? Old Town is empty of extra children, though. Not many people live in the business district. I park in the alley and come in through the back. The store is dark, just like I left it. It's close to nine, and considering her habits lately, I expect my mom to be in bed already. I find her sitting on the couch watching a movie.

She looks over and smiles. "I thought maybe you went to a party tonight that I didn't remember you telling me about."

"No. I kind of forgot it's Halloween."

She pats the cushion next to her.

"What are you watching?"

"I don't know, some Hallmark classic."

I plop onto the couch next to her. "Let me guess, the lady has cancer and the man never knew but always loved her."

"No. I think the little boy is sick and the mom is realizing how much time she's spent at work."

I pull onto me some of the blanket my mom has over her. We don't say anything, just watch the movie, but it's comfortable, familiar, and by the end of the movie, I feel much better. I've missed her. I've missed this.

The next day on my way into the store I brush by the mail carrier, who is on his way out. He nods a hello and I smile. My mom stands behind the counter sifting slowly through the mail. I wonder if she's taking her time to avoid the bills waiting to be paid with money we don't have. When she gets to the end she looks up at me. "Hey."

"Hi."

She holds up the envelopes. "Are you getting nervous?" she asks.

"Yes." If only she knew how much.

"When do you think you'll start hearing?"

"Hearing?"

"From Berkeley, Sac State, San Francisco, you know, colleges?"

"Oh right." I'd have to send in applications first. "Not yet. By April, I think." I knew, actually. I knew the deadline for most colleges was fast approaching. I still hadn't told her my plan to delay for a year or two.

"April? That's so far away."

It feels like it's just around the corner.

She smiles and adds the stack of mail to the drawer then turns to the too-big-for-our-pathetic-schedule calendar on the back counter. She rips off the top month, folding it neatly and tucking it into the cupboard below with the others for future generations to see that we had the most boring year ever. "It's a new month," she tells me. "Time to schedule our lives." She holds her pen poised, ready to put my life back into little defined boxes where it belongs. "Any extra school things this week?"

"No. I have a big test tomorrow, so maybe I should study tonight."

She blocks off tonight after five for me. "I have a

business owners' meeting next Wednesday night."

She writes six o'clock down on the calendar without any other details.

"Where is it?"

"I'm not sure. We rotate stores."

"Then how come we've never hosted one?"

"Our store is way too small for that." She looks at the almost blank calendar. "Anything else?"

My eyes linger on Saturday, the day Xander and I had been doing our career days. It would be his turn. "No. Nothing."

"Wow, we have an exciting month. I don't know if we can handle such a full schedule."

"No birthday parties?"

"Not yet."

She puts away the pen and gets out some cleaning supplies. Throughout the afternoon I find myself staring at the calendar and the Wednesday night "meeting" written there in black. Why am I so suspicious of that? I had been lying to my mom for the past few months about who I was hanging out with. Is it possible she's been lying to me as well? The name Matthew pops into my head and I quickly try to push it out. But it lingers there.

"Mom, who is—"

The bell on the door rings, cutting off my sentence. I look over, some silly false hope inside telling me it could be Xander. It's not. It's Mason.

CHAPTER 22

. . . .

My mom smiles. "Hi. Mason, right?"

She remembers his name?

"Yes. Hi. Nice to see you again. I was hoping I could steal Caymen for an hour or two, if that's all right with you, of course."

"That's perfectly fine. Where are you headed?"

"We have band practice and I wanted her opinion on some songs."

"He doesn't know my opinions on music are worthless yet," I say to my mom.

"She has great opinions," my mom assures him as if he's really worried about it.

He walks by my mom and I see her eyes linger on his calf. She points. "What does it mean?"

He twists his foot to look at his tattoo as though he forgot it was there. "It's a Chinese symbol. It means 'acceptance.'"

"Very beautiful," my mom says.

"Thank you." He turns to me. "You ready?"

"Sure. Thanks, Mom. I'll see you in a while."

He puts his arm around my neck. I'm getting used to Mason's need for human contact. I kind of need human contact right now, too.

I nudge him with my elbow. "You're wearing shorts in November?"

"It's not that cold."

He's right, of course. On the coast of California the beginning of November is fairly similar to the beginning of most months. "Where do you have practice?" I ask.

He points to a purple van.

"In a van?"

"No, we're driving there."

The side door to the van slides open, and Skye climbs out with a smile. "I didn't think he'd be able to talk you out of that store."

"Why not?"

"Because you're so responsible. But he assured me that he could. Apparently I underestimated Tic charm."

More like she underestimated my loneliness. Mason

smells good, and I lean into his chest a little more. "Well, my mom was in a good mood. It was really her that made the decision."

"*Oh!*" Mason says. "Check it out." He opens the passenger-side door and practically dives in, retrieving something off the floor. He brings out a *Starz* magazine. "Another article. You should start collecting them. They're like our claim to fame now, right?"

I grab the magazine and scan the cover until I find Xander under the caption *Xander Spence and Sadie Newel spotted in LA over the weekend.* The picture is him holding hands with a girl who has short dark hair and long tan legs. My stomach twists so tight I want to vomit. So Xander got more than a customer's dress shirt last weekend.

I open to the article and read, "Xander Spence, the son of high-end hotel owner Blaine Spence, was spotted in Los Angeles last weekend outside the nightclub Oxygen with his longtime girlfriend, actress Sadie Newel, who has been filming in Paris for the last six months. . . ."

Longtime girlfriend? I can't read anymore because my vision blurs. There is no way I'm going to cry over this. I had already let Xander go. *I gave back his camera*, I remind myself. That was my release. But secretly, deep down, I had been hoping he would come back around. I bite the inside of my cheeks and force back the tears. "Wow, exciting article," I say. "Two people were seen walking. Now that's news."

Six months. She'd been gone for the last six months filming. I was his distraction. My mind chooses this moment to remind me of how platonic our relationship has been: how he never walked too close, how he pointedly called himself my friend when talking to Mason, how he never called our outings dates. They were "career days." How he hadn't even been by this week. Stupid mind. Why didn't it tell me these things earlier? I had obviously misinterpreted his reactions to things. I feel stupid. He really just wanted to be friends.

I swallow the tears. Good. This is what I need—a clean break. A firm break. I look at the picture of Sadie Newel. She is beautiful and sophisticated and much more his type.

Henry appears from behind the van. "So are we ready to record our first single?" He's holding up his phone. "Xander says the studio is totally free right now."

"Are you okay?" Skye asks quietly. I'm smashed in the middle seat between her and Derrick, the drummer.

"I'm fine. Why wouldn't I be?" And by "fine" I mean freaking out. We are going to see Xander. I am going to have to face him. This is not good. I consider flinging myself out of the van now that this news has sunk in properly.

"Because you just found out the guy you like has a girlfriend." She points to the magazine that had been thrown back into the van and somehow ended up under my foot (I may or may not have purposefully ground my heel into Sadie's perfect face).

"Was it that obvious?"

She shrugs. "Give me some credit. I am your best friend."

"Yeah, well, I'm over him."

"That was fast."

"That's because I've been trying to get over him since the minute I met him so I'm one step ahead of myself."

She pats my knee like she thinks I'm in denial. I am not in denial.

Okay, so I'm totally in denial, but I need her to play along with me until all the feelings I am trying to convince myself I have are actually true.

I'm hoping the studio and Xander aren't a package deal. Because I'm not ready to face him at the moment. It's completely possible that he just called the studio and told them the band was coming. It didn't mean he would be there. At least that's what I tell myself during the fifteen-minute car ride where all the band members are talking excitedly over one another. We drive through a security checkpoint, past a wrought iron gate and onto a tiled drive. The second I see a huge fountain and a house with more windows than I can easily count I realize the studio and Xander are a package deal—they live in the same place.

CHAPTER 23

· · · · · · ·

Xander meets us in the circular drive, and I try to stay hidden at the back of the group. I wonder how embarrassed I should be about my behavior over the last couple of months. Had he sensed my racing heart every time he came around? Had I looked at him with those stupid doe eyes? Skye had picked up on it. He probably had, too. And now he's going to think I asked the band if I could tag along just so I could see him.

"The studio is around the back," Xander says as the guys start to grab their instruments from the van. The sound of his voice makes my eyes sting again. I curse at myself. He continues, "And it's totally up to you, but the studio has its own instruments if you don't want to carry all this."

"Awesome," Mason says, putting his guitar back. Henry shuts the back.

"Follow me," Xander says. It takes him a minute to notice me. I had hidden myself pretty well behind Skye and between the bass player, Mike, and the drummer, Derrick. He furrows his brow. "Hey. I didn't know you were coming."

"I didn't either." I know that sounds squeaky and wrong because my throat is so tight but I try to pretend like I'm perfectly fine.

He hesitates for a second, almost like he wants to say more but says, "Okay, let's go." He gestures for everyone to follow. I realize he expects me to catch up with him, walk next to him. I only know this because he glances over his shoulder a few times as we make the journey through his huge yard, past his built-in pool and basketball court. But I stay where I am, between two almost strangers, listening to them banter back and forth. I'm going to prove to him that I know we're just friends. That we were always just friends. Not only that, but that I have other friends, too, and he doesn't have to worry about me throwing myself at him.

"Okay, guys," he says, opening the door and setting

his keys and cell phone on the small table to the left. "Get comfortable with the toys. I'll fire up the equipment." The band immediately attacks the instruments while Xander stays on this side of the large glass window and starts messing with slides and buttons. Skye floats onto a couch behind Xander and I join her.

Xander shuts both the door that leads to the outside and the one that leads to where the band members are already playing, effectively shutting out the sound. He smiles at me on the way back to his seat, and I'm mad that my heart hasn't gotten the update yet about his girlfriend because his smile still sends it racing.

"There are some sodas and things in the fridge if you ladies are thirsty." He points to a stainless steel fridge in the corner then turns, holds a headset to one ear, pushes a button on the panel in front of him, and says into a microphone, "Go ahead and run through the song a few times, and I'll let you know when we're ready to record."

He lets go of the button and spins in his twisty chair to face us. It would be so much easier if Xander were less . . . less what? Confident? Attractive? Flirty?

Yes, that last one would be nice. No matter what my brain had reminded me, Xander is a flirt. If he were my boyfriend and he was hanging out with a girl like he had been with me, I would be angry.

"What?" Xander asks.

"What?"

"You're staring at me."

"I am not," I say.

"You were. Wasn't she?" he asks Skye.

"Yeah, you were."

"Well, I'm trying to decide what you have to live for."

"Excuse me?"

I gesture around this amazing studio that is sitting in his *backyard*. "How do you manage to get out of bed every day with such a depressing future?"

"Actually, someone is working with me on that very problem. I hope she can help me figure out what my future holds." That statement makes me remember why we had started hanging out in the first place. We were in the "same" situation, according to him. Maybe he just thought I understood him better than most. I didn't. We were complete opposites.

The door to the band room opens, and Mason sling-shots himself out and flies across Skye's and my lap, laying his head in mine. "I think we're ready," he says to Xander.

"Okay." Xander waits for a moment, probably thinking Mason is going to get up, then he nods his head toward Mason's calf. "Nice tattoo."

"Thanks. Speaking of." Mason looks at me, grabbing a strand of my hair and twirling it around his finger. I'm grateful for his attention. It makes me feel less stupid about how I'd been acting with Xander. Like he'll see I wasn't just pining away for him. "Was your mom being sarcastic today or do you think she really likes it?"

"My mom isn't the sarcastic type."

Mason laughs. "Really? Then how did you master the art so well? Is your dad super sarcastic?"

As if sensing the worst topic anybody could ever bring up has been introduced, the entire band joins us in the room that already feels sweltering. My chest tightens with a longing to say, "I have no idea if my dad is sarcastic because I've never met the man."

"She wouldn't know," Skye says, not helping matters at all.

"Really?" Mason asks. "You don't know your dad? What's the story there?"

I shift, wondering how I can joke my way out of this topic.

Xander looks at his watch. "Guys, I'm on a schedule here. Let's get this thing pounded out." He catches my eye for a split second, proving he did that just for me.

Mason rolls off the couch seeming to forget my dad as easily as he brought him up. I wish I could forget him that easily.

The band plays in front of us, like a silent movie, Xander wearing the headphones and making adjustments on the knobs and slides. I'm not sure what those adjustments do, but he obviously knows. Skye stands and helps herself to a soda from the fridge. "Want one?" she asks.

"I'm good."

She rejoins me on the couch. "How're you doing?"

"Fine."

"I get it, by the way."

"Get what?"

"Him. I get why you like him. There's something about him." She points at Xander's back. Even though we're not talking very loud and Xander has the headphones on I want to shush her.

"I told you. It's over. His girlfriend is an actress, Skye."

She rolls her eyes. "Actresses are overrated. Fight for him."

I stand, needing to work off some nervous energy. "It's not a competition when one person has already won."

Xander's phone rings from where it sits on the table next to the door. He obviously doesn't hear it because he doesn't react at all. I'm standing less than five feet from his phone, so I give in to my curiosity and look at the glowing screen. The picture is what I see first: a dark-haired girl laughing. I don't need to see the name at the bottom to know what it will say, but I look anyway. Sadie. "See . . . ?" I say, raising one eyebrow at Skye.

"Seriously?" she says.

I nod and then, while looking at Xander's back and the band still going strong behind the glass, I act on the strangest impulse ever, scoop up his phone, and answer it. "Hello?"

Skye's mouth opens so wide that I fear her jaw might come unhinged.

"Hello? . . . Xander? . . . I can't hear you very well. I'm in the car." Her voice sounds so normal. I had seen Sadie Newel in a few movies, and this version didn't sound like the sophisticated version from the theater.

I don't know what to say now that I've done it. "This isn't Xander. Let me get him for you."

"I can't hear you. What? Ugh. Listen, my connection is bad, but I need you to work your magic. I'll call you back when I get to the hotel." The phone goes dead, and I push it back onto the table as though it's about to explode.

Skye giggles. "You're crazy."

"She didn't know it was me. She's calling back later."

Xander spins in his chair, making me gasp. "Does anyone want to listen?" he asks, taking off the headphones and holding them out.

"Yes." Skye jumps up and moves forward. When she's settled into the chair next to Xander's listening to the band he spins around to face me.

"So why not this?" I ask, sitting on the couch again.

"What?"

"Why wouldn't you produce music for a living? It seems like a passion of yours."

He rolls the chair forward until our knees bump. "My father would never front the money for something like that."

I stare at our knees, wondering if I should use the wheels on his chair to my advantage and shove him away. I ignore the urge. "But he built this studio?"

"My older brother is a classical guitarist. This was to provide a creative outlet. A hobby. I spent a lot of time in here with him learning this stuff. But this is not a career in my father's opinion."

"I thought you didn't care what your father thought," I say.

He narrows his eyes as if considering the question. "I guess I care what my father's money thinks." He rubs the back of his neck. "Without it I can't be free of him. It's like a double-edged sword."

I get what he's saying: that he needs money to go to college, get his own career, so he can make his own money. But I wonder if Xander really only cares about the money. He seems to put a lot of effort into making his father angry. I'm guessing he cares a lot about what his father thinks.

On the other side of the glass Mason sings with his eyes closed. He looks ridiculous.

Xander taps my knee with a closed fist, bringing my

attention back to him. "I'm glad you're here. I didn't think . . ."

I tilt my head, waiting for him to finish.

"After last Saturday . . . and you returned my camera without a word. . . ." His eyes bore into mine.

"What?" I ask, dying to know why he's not finishing his thoughts. What he's leaving unsaid. Did how we left things bother him as much as they did me?

"I'm out of town this weekend but next Saturday? Are we still on?"

I blink once. That's what he wants? More career days?

Skye lets out a yelp, startling me. "That was so awesome." She stands.

Xander stands as well, walks over, and pushes the Mic button. "That's a wrap. Good job, guys." He goes to the table and pockets his keys and cell then looks at me apologetically. "I didn't know you were coming. I really am on a tight schedule." He checks his watch. "I'm supposed to be at the airport in twenty minutes."

"I'm pretty sure we can walk ourselves to the car."

"So I'll see you next Saturday?"

I want to say, "I don't know, you better check with your girlfriend first. She just called; should we ask her?" But I don't. I just nod. Because girlfriend or not, I want to see him on Saturday. Apparently I'm further from being over him than I hoped and I hate myself for being so weak.

CHAPTER 24

• • • • • • •

Monday morning as I say good-bye to my mom and grab my backpack for school there's a knock on the door. I look over to see Xander standing there holding his two cups. My heart jumps to my throat. No, no, no, no, no. This can't be happening. He has a girlfriend. If I knew . . . My heart doubles its speed when he smiles. If more than my heart knew that we have something, I could open that door right now and face disappointing my mother.

"Who's that?"

This is not a good time for this. My mom and I finally feel right again. I shake my head no, but instead of walking away Xander holds up a drink with a smirk as if to say, *I'm not leaving so let me in.*

I narrow my eyes and smile a little. All right, if he wants to play it that way. Game on. "Oh, that looks like Mrs. Dalton's grandson. He came in the other day to pick up a doll for her. I'll just tell him we don't open until nine today and to come back later."

"Oh no, honey. Mrs. Dalton is our best customer. Why don't you let him in and see what he needs."

Or there's that. Crap.

I slowly unlock the door. "Hi," I say when I open it. His familiar scent wafts in with the breeze and doesn't help my already racing heart. I take a deep breath. "We're not open yet. Did your grandma need something?"

He takes a sip of the drink then hands it to me. I cringe. That act alone is going to make my mom think he is the most obnoxious rich person in the world who wants me to hold his drink while he shops.

"I want to meet your mom," he says loud enough for her to hear.

"Yes, my mom is much more knowledgeable about the dolls than I am." I turn toward my mother. "Mom, he . . . um . . . I'm sorry, what was your name again? Wellington or something?"

A crease of confusion forms between his brows, but I can tell he also thinks it's funny.

"No, that wasn't your name. Um . . ."

"Xander."

"Right. I knew it was something odd like that."

"Caymen," my mom says. "Sorry, my daughter is very dry. She's just kidding."

"Last time Xander came in he was really interested in the sleeping baby dolls. Didn't you say they made your heart happy just to look at them?"

"I don't recall saying that but it sounds like me."

I laugh then quickly suck in my lips to stop myself. "Maybe you could show him our collection, Mom."

My mom tilts her head at me, obviously confused. She's going to call me out. She must sense I know Xander. I need to get out of here. I shake the full cup of hot chocolate in my hand, pretending it's empty. "There's a trash outside. I'll just take care of this for you." I turn back to my mom. "I'm going to be late. I'll see you after school."

"Have a great day, honey."

I leave, flashing Xander a look of wide-eyed innocence. A sadness follows me out of the store, and I can't decide if it's because I just lied to my mom again or because I really do want my mom to know Xander. Not just know him but like him.

I'm ten steps from school when a pair of hands grabs my arms from behind, stopping me in my tracks. "You are the biggest brat. You know that, right?" Xander says in my ear. He lets go and I turn around, smiling.

"No, you are. I told you I didn't want you to meet my mom yet. But you thought you'd do it anyway."

"Yes, I did. I wanted to show you that all moms like me. And your mom is no exception: she loves me."

My heart skips a beat. "Really?"

"I didn't know it was going to cost me a hundred and fifty bucks to prove it but she's smitten."

Oh. Of course she loved him. He was a customer. "You bought a doll?" He isn't holding a bag so I grab the lapels of his open jacket and look inside.

"It's not *on* me, woman. I put it in the car."

"Who did you buy?"

"You don't honestly expect me to remember."

"I *know* you remember."

"Daphne."

"You bought a Wailer?"

"Yes, I was feeling a little frustrated in there, and this screaming baby represented my mood very well. I'll just give her to my grandma next year for her birthday." He looks down. "You thought I stashed the doll in my coat?"

I realize I'm still holding tight to his jacket. "If your ego fits in there anything is possible." Just as I'm about to let go, he puts his hands over mine, sandwiching them between his chest and his warm hands.

I'm now staring at the open collar of his name-brand shirt, trying to pretend that he's not staring at me. Classmates walk by me, rushing to get to class, and I sense them looking at me.

"I thought you were out of town."

He shrugs a little. "I'm back."

"I thought we weren't seeing each other until Saturday." My voice comes out breathy.

"I couldn't wait."

My heart pounds loudly in my ears. "Whatever happened the other night, anyway?"

"With what?" he asks softly. Or maybe I can't hear him because of the whole heart-pounding thing.

"The hotel crisis of the decade. Did you find a replacement shirt?"

"Yes. One trip down to LA is all it took."

Right. LA, the place where he saw Sadie Newel. My good mood leaves quickly. "Is that all?"

He nods and I'm about to pull my hands away when he says, "Come to the benefit with me?"

"What?"

"It's in two weeks. There'll be dancing, schmoozing, sucking people dry of their money. It's for my mom's charity."

"Another career day?"

"No."

I meet his eyes. Isn't that something he should take his

girlfriend to? "I have plans that night."

"Doing what?"

"Avoiding a benefit." I smile. "I better go. I'm really late." Why aren't my feet moving?

"Bye, Caymen." He lets go of my hands.

I drop mine to my sides but then surprise myself by giving him a hug. He hugs me back, and I linger there longer than I should. Why can't I just walk away from Xander Spence and not look back? The tardy bell rings behind me.

"I gotta go." I push away and turn to leave.

"Caymen," he says, stopping me.

I turn back. "Yeah."

"The employee who doesn't know how to use an iron?"

"Yeah."

"He wasn't fired. I know that bothered you so I . . . He wasn't fired."

Why does this news make me want to cry? "Good. Maybe he should attend the next career day I host where we'll learn how to properly iron all your T-shirts."

"I'll extend the invite."

That afternoon as I'm sitting behind the register doing homework and my mom is wiping down counters, she chuckles.

"What?" I ask.

"Mrs. Dalton's grandson."

"Xander?"

"Yes, Xander. He was funny this morning."

"Oh yeah?" I ask hopefully. Maybe he really did make a good impression on my mom. Maybe it wouldn't bother her after all to know we hang out.

"I don't believe he wanted you to throw away his trash. And then, after you left, he was telling me how much he liked your name and how he had just been to the Cayman Islands last year. He asked how often I went as though everyone in the world goes wherever they want whenever they want."

I'm usually the one making fun of the rich and she's the one telling me to watch myself. For years it made me angry because I knew she felt the same way. And now Xander is the one she chooses to pick on? A lump forms in my throat and I don't think I can talk through it. I try anyway. "He seemed nice, though."

She shrugs.

Every defensive bone in my body is shaking.

"Are you seeing Mason today?"

Her abrupt change in subject renders me speechless.

"I really like the sentiment of his tattoo. I'm not a huge fan of tattoos in general—they are just so permanent—but I like its message."

"Acceptance?" I ask, waiting for her to realize how

ironic that is after what she had just said.

"Yes, a beautiful message. I'm sure he meets a lot of people that don't accept him at face value. I'm so proud of you for being able to look beyond that."

"Beyond what exactly, Mom? His skin color?"

"What? No. This has nothing to do with his skin color. Geez, Caymen, what do you think I'm talking about?"

"I don't know; that's what I'm trying to figure out." I know what she's talking about—his lip ring, his tattoo, his tic—but I'm too irritated to give her a break. Can she really not see the hypocrisy in what she's saying?

"I'm going to do my homework upstairs."

"Okay."

I make it to the door when it hits me—she suspects there's something going on between me and Xander. That's why she said what she did. Why she put down Xander and built up Mason. It's her subtle way of steering me the way she wants me to go. That has to be it. I want to turn around and ask her if I'm right. But what does it matter when he has a girlfriend?

Upstairs I pass the counter on the way toward my bedroom and see another pink-enveloped bill. All my irritation is immediately coupled with worry. I'm not sure which emotion is worse.

CHAPTER 25

• • • • • • •

look through the rack at the Salvation Army with Skye, trying not to think too hard.

Skye sighs. "I guess I just don't understand what happened."

"What's there to understand? He has a girlfriend. I'm pretty sure that's the end of the story." I haven't seen him in a few days and whenever he's away I'm able to think more clearly about things.

"But the way he looks at you is just . . ." She stops, maybe realizing this isn't helping matters at all. "I'm sorry. Moving on." She holds up a shirt and raises her eyebrows at me.

"Not your color."

She puts it back. "Speaking of moving on, what about Tic? He totally likes you."

"Mason likes whoever is in front of him at the moment."

"Okay, so he has the attention span of an insect, but I think he could settle down." She holds up another shirt and I nod, so she adds it to the growing stack over her arm. "He really is an amazing guy if you get to know him. They're performing at The Beach tomorrow. It's a big deal for them. You should come."

I should go. Mason really is a good fit for me. My mom likes him; my best friend likes him; I know I could've liked him by now, too, if someone else wasn't in the way.

My hand stops on the black dress. The one I had found when I was here with Xander. I'm surprised it's still here. It's amazing. I pull it out and run one hand along the hand-sewn beading.

Skye gasps. "That is gorgeous."

I put it back on the rack and move the next piece of clothing, a hideous spandex jumpsuit, in front of it.

"Oh no way," Skye says, coming to my side and freeing the dress. "You are so getting this."

"No."

"Yes."

"Why? Where would I ever wear it?"

"That's not the point. You find something like this and you buy it. This is the kind of dress you plan an event around."

I bite my lip. "I don't have forty dollars."

"I do. I'm buying it for you. It will be my I'm-sorry-you-got-screwed-over-by-a-rich-guy gift."

I laugh a little. "I'll pay you back."

Skye was right. The Beach (a club that named itself way too literally) is a much bigger venue and I'm amazed by how many people have shown up to hear Crusty Toads play. The waves roll in behind the huge stage, and the salty wind only adds to the performance. It's a great concert, but I'm already planning my early-exit strategy. It's not like we're going to get to talk to the band after the show with this many people vying for their attention.

Skye has made some awful flattened-toad T-shirts, and I am wearing one against my better judgment.

"Two more songs and I need to go," I yell to Skye as Mason sings in his honey-smooth voice.

"I knew you would try to leave early so I made plans for us after the show."

"Plans? What do you mean?"

She nods her head up to the stage. "The guys want to hang out."

I glance up at Mason and he catches my eye. He sings right at me for two lines and I can see how girls might stalk him after something like that. My heart stutters. "Okay. I'll stay."

Skye giggles. "Of course you will."

When the last song is over I expect Mason to disappear behind the stage for a while like he did after the last concert I went to. He doesn't. He drops his microphone, jumps off the stage, and weaves through grasping hands and straight to me.

By the time he reaches me my heart is in my throat.

"Hi." That single word is said with so much rasp and emotion that I realize why he's such a good performer.

"Hi."

He takes my hand and squeezes. "Don't leave."

"Okay."

Then he does. He heads back to the stage and slips around it, through a line of burly men and out of sight. I watch him the entire way and then shake myself out of the trance when he's gone.

"Told you he's crazy about you."

I come back to my senses and see that the little stunt drew a lot of attention. So many people are staring at me. "I need some water," I say.

"Will you get me a soda?" she asks, and hands me a five.

I tromp through the sand in my bare feet, wondering why I didn't just leave my shoes in the car instead of checking them in. They were going to take forever to collect. A guy sitting at the bar looks vaguely familiar. And considering he's staring at me as I walk up, he must recognize me as well. I can't place him, though, and my mind scans through all my classes at school. I can tell his brain is performing a similar task when finally his eyes light up with recognition. Now he has the advantage because I still can't place him.

"Xander's little friend, right?" His remark reeks of arrogance.

The moment he says it I realize he's Robert from the restaurant. The one I thought had called me a stray. I'm beginning to think Xander covered for him. "Yes. Hi." I lean into the bar and order bottled water and a soda.

When the bartender turns around to fill my order, Robert asks, "Did Xander get you in here tonight?"

I narrow my eyes. Now that Xander's not here I don't feel the need to be as polite. "No. I know the band. How did *you* get in?" I pick up my drinks from the counter.

Robert laughs and gives me a once-over. "I see the appeal. You have great . . . eyes. When Xander gets bored of slumming it with you we should get together."

I never thought I had the dumping-soda-on-someone-purposefully instinct, but sure enough my hand reacts automatically. But he has instincts, too. Probably born from a lifetime of people wanting to dump soda on him. His hand darts out and grabs my wrist.

"Not a good idea," he tells me, a few drops of soda spilling over the side. "This shirt cost more than your monthly rent."

"Too bad you had to sell your soul to afford it."

"Everything okay?" Mason comes up from behind, wrapping his arms around my waist.

I'm just about to murder someone is all. "Let's go."

"You get around," Robert calls after me. It takes everything in me not to throw the glass at him, soda and all.

"Who was that?" Mason asks as we walk away.

"Nobody worth ever thinking about again."

Only I can't stop thinking about him. He's Xander's *friend*. Is that how Xander acts when I'm not around? I'm seething.

"Caymen?" Mason takes my bottled water from me and grabs my hand. "Do I need to beat that guy up?"

I hold on to him tightly. "No. Not worth it," I tell myself again. But I know this isn't about Robert anymore. And I'm trying to decide if that advice still applies.

CHAPTER 26

• • • • • • •

The next night I decide I need to finish up the website I had been slowly putting together over the last few weeks. I pull the pictures up on the computer. Unfortunately for me, along with the dolls, all the photos of Xander from the hotel room photo shoot open as well. Even in a photo his smile has a softening effect on me.

I scroll through them, lingering on the ones where I had made him laugh. In that magazine picture of him with Sadie Newel he hadn't even been smiling. She probably can't make him laugh. I let out a frustrated grunt. *Who cares, Caymen? He is with her.* I try to delete the pictures of him but can't bring myself to do it. Instead I group all the doll pictures into a file and open that so I don't have to look at Xander's amber eyes anymore.

I add names and prices beneath the dolls.

"Is that a new ordering site?" my mom asks, coming into the kitchen.

"No." I smile. I had planned on surprising her when the site was all finished, but it's getting close and I need to make up for the attitude I've been giving her lately. I switch from the pictures to the website layout. "I've been working on something for the store."

She positions herself behind me. On the screen is a banner that says, "Dolls and More." I had thought about taking out the "and more," but it feels like tradition now. And maybe we could add "more" once it gets up and running. I scan down a little to where it has my mom's name and her contact information. "I want to add a picture of you here. Maybe we can take one out front or something next to the window display."

"What is this?" she asks.

"It's a website I'm designing for the store." I put my hands out to the sides and say, "Surprise," in a false screaming voice.

"A website." Her voice is low and even.

"It's going to be great, Mom. It will pump up our business, get us more sales. It's the next step to our growth."

"No." That's all she says and then turns and rounds the counter into the kitchen.

I'm confused. "No?"

She pulls down a glass from the cupboard and fills it with water from the tap. "I don't want a website."

Even though we don't have cable or cell phones or even a newer computer, it's not because my mom thinks technology is the devil or anything. It's really just because we can't afford it. "It's cheap, Mom. Less than twenty dollars a year for the domain name and I can run it. You could even run it once we get it going. It's really easy and—"

"I said no, Caymen. I don't want it."

"Why?"

"Because I said so."

"That's not an answer, Mom; that's a conversation ender."

"Good, because this conversation has ended." She slams the glass onto the counter and I'm surprised when it doesn't shatter. Then she marches out of the kitchen and into her room.

I close the pages I had open on the computer, trying to remain calm. What I really want to do is shove the computer to the floor. I don't. I turn off the screen and walk slowly downstairs and outside. Then I run. I don't stop until my cheeks are numb and my lungs feel close to bursting and my legs ache.

By the time I get back to the store I'm dripping sweat and I need to talk this through with someone. I pick up the phone and dial Skye's number. It goes directly to voice mail. My fingers tap an impatient rhythm on the wall and I decide not to leave a message.

I should call Mason. I don't.

I grab the binder from beneath the counter and plop it on top of our oversize calendar. I find Mrs. Dalton's phone number.

I almost chicken out as I listen to the phone ring.

"Hello," Mrs. Dalton answers.

"Hi . . ." *I have the wrong number.* I gasp when I realize it's past nine o'clock. Was she in bed? "Sorry to call so late. This is Caymen . . . from the doll store."

"It's not late at all, and I only know one Caymen," she says. "How are you?"

"I'm fine."

"Did I order something? I don't remember, but that doesn't mean I didn't."

"Like you'd forget if you ordered something," I say.

"That's true. Then you're checking to see if I've died? I may look old, but I'm only sixty-seven."

"Really? And here I thought you were in your forties."

"Nice try."

I take a breath. "I was hoping I could get a phone number from you. I think he would give it to me himself. . . .

I guess what I mean is that I'm not trying to get it behind his back or anything. He's even called me before. I don't think he'd mind if I had it."

"Take a deep breath, honey."

"I'm sorry."

"You would like Alex's phone number? He is quite the charmer, isn't he?"

"No. I mean, well, yes, he is, but we're just friends." And right now I need a friend.

"That's what it sounds like."

I laugh. Mrs. Dalton is funny.

"Yes, let me get it for you. I have this fancy phone that can store hundreds of numbers, but I still write them in my little red book."

I realize I'm holding my breath in anticipation.

"Are you ready?" she asks.

More than ready. "Yes." I write down the number on the calendar. "Thanks so much."

"No problem. Tell him I said hi."

I hang up and stare at the number for an eternity. I want to talk to him. I need to talk to him. But my insides are all twisted up. I squeeze my eyes closed, and when I open them again I dial the number quickly before I change my mind. It rings three times and I feel like minutes pass between each one.

Finally he answers.

CHAPTER 27

• • • • • • •

"Hello." His familiar voice automatically eases my tension. He's nothing like Robert. If he were he'd have been gone the minute he found out I lived above a doll store. I relax with this thought.

"Alex?" I don't know why Alex came out of my mouth. Probably because I had written that name next to his phone number when Mrs. Dalton called him that.

"Caymen?"

"Yeah. Hi."

"Alex?" he asks.

"Sorry. Slip. I was talking to your grandma."

"Why wouldn't you be?"

I lie on the floor behind the register and feel a bit like Skye as I stare at the ceiling. This position is conducive to thinking. No wonder why she spends so much time here.

It's silent for a long time before he says, "Did you need something?"

You. "I've needed my morning hot chocolate, but someone got me addicted to it then took it away."

"Is that your subtle way of saying you missed me last week?"

"I've missed hot chocolate. I just think of you as the guy who brings it to me. Sometimes I forget your name and call you hot chocolate guy."

He laughs a little, and I find myself wishing I could see his face so I could witness how his eyes light up when he smiles.

"And I've missed your wit."

"Understandable." My heart beats heavily in my temples. "I never said thank you for letting me borrow the camera."

"So does this mean you're done with the website? What's the address? I want to see the soul-sucking dolls on my screen." Some papers shuffle on his end and I wonder if he's reaching across a desk or something to get on his computer.

"No. I mean, there is no address. My mom doesn't want it."

"Oh. Why?"

"I'm not sure, actually. I was going to surprise her, show her what I'd done, and she flipped out on me. Totally shut down, said she didn't want it. It was so unlike her."

"What did you put on it?"

"That's the thing. I'd only shown her the banner and our contact info. I was telling her how I wanted to put her picture up as well."

"Is she camera shy?"

I prop my feet up on the wall and let my free hand drift above my head. "No."

"Maybe she just doesn't want that on the internet, her face along with where you live. It's basically like you're posting your address on the website along with her face. I can see why that might freak her out, a bunch of strangers knowing where you live. Is there a way to do it without the personal info?"

I had stopped breathing. I know this only because black edges into my vision. I take a breath. Is she worried about a bunch of strangers finding out where we live or one very specific person? My father.

"You okay?"

I hum, not trusting my voice. My whole throat is tight.

I'm not sure words could make it through at all.

"You sure?"

I swallow. "Yes. I think you might be right." Considering how much my throat hurts, I'm surprised by how normal my voice sounds.

"I often am."

"Do you think he's tried?" It takes me a moment to realize I'd said that out loud and another moment to realize that Xander has responded back and is now waiting for my answer to a question I didn't hear. "What?"

"I said, 'do I think who's tried what?'"

I force myself to sit up and then stand. Lying down was making my thoughts too free. "These strangers you refer to. Do you think they'd try to find us for their sinister purposes?"

"What sinister purposes are those?"

I lean against the back counter and with a black pen doodle around his phone number I had written on the calendar. "You know, the things strangers need people for . . . eating their candy and finding their lost dogs."

"I don't buy it, you know."

"You shouldn't. Those are their ploys to lure you into the car so they can take you away. I'm glad you wouldn't fall for it."

"I'm talking about your humor. I know that sometimes you use it to hide things."

"You give me way too much credit. I really am as shallow as I seem."

"Hardly. And the answer to your question is yes. Yes, I think your father has tried to find you. What father wouldn't want to know his daughter?"

"The kind that would run away at even the thought of me." I don't know why I'm talking about this. There's a reason I avoid this subject. It feels as though someone has poked every inch of my skin with a needle, leaving me raw and exposed.

"If he had known you he'd have never been able to leave."

I close my eyes. What kind of man could run away like that? Just leave my mom in that state. The kind that was scared out of his mind. Scared what I would do to his future. I did ruin futures: my mom is evidence of that. He was just a kid, really, with a future so full of possibilities and the money to make it happen. He probably was a lot like Xander. Which is why when my mom saw Xander she couldn't help but see her past. "Could you have left?"

"Never."

I can't decide if that makes me feel better or worse.

"That's what makes me think he's tried, Caymen. A regret like that doesn't go away."

Assuming he regrets it at all. "How hard can one girl be to find?"

"Maybe your mom hasn't told you about his attempts."

"My mom wouldn't keep something like that from me." As I say that my eyes collide with the box on the calendar where she had written "small business association meeting." Maybe she was keeping something like that from me. And if she was, then maybe Xander was right. Maybe she was keeping a lot of things from me. "What are you doing Wednesday night?"

"I'm pretty open."

"Career day. Six thirty. Meet me here."

"It's my turn for career day. I have something planned for tomorrow, remember?"

"Okay, fine. Tomorrow you. Wednesday me." I clear my throat. "Unless that's too much. You aren't going to get in trouble for seeing me so much, right?" I want to add, "Girlfriends can get so jealous," but I don't because I'm afraid it might sound bitter. That's the last thing I want to come off as.

"No, of course not. I already told you my parents like you."

I don't doubt that anymore now that I know his parents don't think he's dating me. "Tomorrow afternoon would be better than morning for me."

"How about two?"

"Sounds good. I'll see you tomorrow, then."

"Caymen?"

"Yeah?"

"You don't have to hang up. If you need to talk some more I have time."

The knot in my stomach loosens with the suggestion, and just as I'm about to open my mouth a girl's voice sounds on his end.

"Xander, what's taking so long? Are you on the phone?"

"Yes, sorry to make you wait. I'll be right down. Give me five minutes."

"Who're you talking to?" she asks.

"A friend." A door shuts and then his voice is louder in the receiver. "Sorry about that."

"That's okay. Sounds like you have to go. I'll see you tomorrow at two. Bye." I hang up before he can stop me, proud my voice sounded casual because it feels like someone has their hands clamped around my throat. No more phone calls. They don't help.

CHAPTER 28

• • • • • • •

I wait on the curb. Every minute that passes after two
o'clock feels like an eternity. I think that maybe he's
changed his mind. Maybe Sadie Newel told him he
couldn't talk to friends late at night and take them on
"career days."

At 2:07 his car rounds the corner. He parks and steps
out.

"Hi," he says.

"Hi." My body still reacts to him like it always has,
my heart picking up speed, tingles spreading through my
arms and up my neck.

He looks over my shoulder to the shop and then back to me. "You ready?"

I nod.

He lifts a hand to my elbow. "Are you okay?"

I meet his eyes and want to say, "No, I still feel like crap. My mom is keeping secrets, I'll probably be homeless in a month, my dad ran out on me, and you have a girlfriend we're both pretending doesn't exist."

I just say, "Yeah, why wouldn't I be?"

He must not believe me because he pulls me into a hug. I close my eyes and breathe him in.

"I'm here," he says into my hair.

"For how long?" I want to ask. "You're a good friend," I say instead, and then untwist myself from his arms.

The ride is a quiet one until Xander pulls into the airport.

"Um . . ." I watch a plane take off then turn my shocked gaze on Xander. "Are we flying somewhere?"

"You're not afraid of flying, are you?"

"I don't think so."

"You've never been on a plane before?"

"No." And maybe I am afraid because my palms start to sweat.

"Really?" He studies me for a moment as though trying to figure out a puzzle.

"You know I told my mom I'd be back tonight, right?"

"Yes. You will be."

"Okay."

It wouldn't have surprised me if Xander stepped into the cockpit of the private jet we boarded and started up the engines. But, thankfully, he didn't. There was a pilot waiting for us.

We settle into seats that face each other. He grabs a bottle of water from a cabinet beneath his seat, takes a sip, and hands it to me. Then he retrieves one for himself.

"Pre-sipped beverages? This flight is so accommodating."

I'm rewarded with a smile. It doesn't last long enough, though, and I try to think of something else to say to bring it back. It's a good distraction, and I've missed his smile. I should tell him that. I don't.

His attention is on the screen of his cell phone and he starts texting or writing an email or something. I slip off my shoes and bring one foot beneath me, trying to get comfortable, trying to forget I'm sitting on a plane that's about to be airborne.

He shifts over a little and pats the space next to him. "You can put your feet up here."

"You don't have a feet phobia?"

"Does such a thing exist?"

"Sure, it's a real condition. There are groups, therapists, the whole nine yards." I slide my feet onto the seat next to him, my ankle brushing against his thigh. "No shallowness of breath? No rapidly beating heart?"

He rests one hand on my foot as he continues to mess with his phone. His eyes meet mine in amusement. "Are those the indicators? I might have an issue after all."

Why does he have to say stuff like that? Before him, I thought I knew if a guy was flirting with me. But he says things so subtly, so smoothly, that it's hard to tell if it's purposeful or if he's just playing along with my jokes.

Maybe I should just ask him, straight out. *What does your girlfriend think of me?* That's a fair question. "Xander?"

"Yes?"

"What . . ."

He puts his phone down and gives me his full attention.

"What are you doing on your phone? Words With Friends or something?" I'm such a wimp. Once it's out in the open, maybe he'll start treating me like he has a girlfriend.

And that's not what I want. This is a problem.

He laughs a little. "No. I'm looking at some proposals for the website before I lose my connection. I'm sorry, though. I'll get off. I'm being rude."

"No. It's fine." The engines outside the window start up and I go tense.

He puts his phone away and grabs hold of my ankle. "The worst part is taking off. Once we're in the sky it's painless."

"What about landing?"

"Okay, the second worst part is taking off."

The cabin lights dim and the plane lurches forward, heading toward the runway. Xander's thumb draws patterns around my ankle. I should be nervous about the plane, but all the nerve endings in my leg are buzzing with his touch. I watch the lights go by as the plane picks up speed, then close my eyes as the pressure of the takeoff pushes me back against the seat. As we level off in the air I relax.

He releases my ankle. "See. Easy as can be."

"Now we just have to land."

"Exactly."

I look around. "There are bathrooms on planes, right? That's not just in the movies?"

He points behind me. When I stand and start to move past him the plane hits some turbulence and sends me off balance. I catch myself on Xander's shoulders.

"I pay them well to do that at just the right time," he says. His not-flirting is really irritating.

I am inches from being in his lap. I'd just have to relax my legs a little and I'd be sitting on him. The temptation to do just that is very real. He steadies me with a hand to my waist, only he doesn't push to help me back up. He just leaves it there against my waist and meets my eyes.

Now my throat is tight for different reasons. And then the plane jerks again, and it might have been my imagination, or my weak legs, but I could've sworn that instead of bracing me with that hand on my waist, he actually pulled me forward. Because now I am in his lap, my hands still on his shoulders.

"Hi," he says.

"Sorry."

"For what?"

"For the fact that you are such a big flirt."

He laughs. "You're the one in my lap. I was just sitting here minding my own business."

"Just the plane, then?"

"Of course."

I try to stand up, but he pulls me back down again.

"Man, the plane is really bumpy today," he says.

"Funny." Only it's not funny at all. A surge of anger goes through me. He has a girlfriend and he is a huge flirt. I don't want to be the dirty little secret. If that's what he thinks I am, he has another thing coming. "Let me up."

He must sense the seriousness that has taken over my voice because this time he helps me stand. I shut myself in the bathroom long enough to regain my composure. After tonight I need to be done with Xander Spence. I say it in my head and then again out loud to the mirror. "I am done with Xander Spence." I'm so convincing that I almost believe myself.

I return to my seat.

"Are you cold? Hot? Hungry?" he asks.

"No, I'm good."

"The seat leans back if you want to sleep or anything."

"Is this a long flight?"

"No, about an hour."

I can't figure out how far an hour will take us from our current location. In a car that wouldn't get us past Oakland, but in the air it's different.

"Any conclusions?" he asks.

"What?"

"Have you figured out where we're going based on your amazing observation skills?"

"No." It bothers me that he knows me well enough to know I was evaluating that very thing. I lean my seat back and pretend to sleep the rest of the flight. Due to my newfound determination I have to suffer the landing without his help.

"That's my brother," he says, pointing to the guy waving at us as we exit the plane onto the tarmac. I turn around and try to get back on the plane. "Oh stop," he says, grabbing my hand. "You'll like him."

"Lucas." They embrace with a single pat to the back. "This is Caymen Meyers."

Lucas turns to me and shakes my hand, a sincerity in his smile. And that's the other thing that's weirding me out. Friend or not, why does his family act like this is so normal? Like they don't care that Xander picked up some girl off the street and is now hanging out with her, flying her around in the family's private jet? Something isn't adding up.

Lucas and Xander start catching up on life as though they haven't seen each other in months. Maybe they haven't.

"Is Dad making you fly home for the benefit?" Xander asks as we come to a black SUV parked on the street.

Lucas sighs. He doesn't look at all like Xander. His hair is blond, while Xander's is brown. His complexion is fair, while Xander's is olive. But they both have the same air about them. "Yes. Do you think I could hire a body double?"

"You know this is Mom's baby. I talked once at the breakfast table about how I was dreading it and she almost broke down in tears. Now I pretend like it is the most exciting thing ever. That works better." Xander opens the passenger-side door and waits like he expects me to get in the front. I smile. "You can sit by your brother." I open the back and climb in.

"Mom just stresses," Lucas says when we've all taken our seats.

"I know."

"Is Scarlett going because I don't know if I can put up with her this year?"

"I don't know. She was at our house last night and didn't say anything. I'm sure Mom tried to convince her. She talked to Mom and Dad without me for a while." Xander glances my way and smiles, and I realize Scarlett must've been the girl who interrupted our phone call last night, not Sadie. "But I'm sure she'll have some gossip about everyone at the benefit. She's like our own personal source of awful information. It wouldn't be the same without her."

Lucas looks over his shoulder at me. "We shouldn't talk about it like this or we'll scare poor Caymen. Don't worry. You'll like it. Lots of creepy old men who will want to dance with you. Lots of food that looks like it might crawl off your plate. And the band is so exciting they don't even need a lead singer."

"I'm in that band. I'm glad you like it," I say.

Lucas stutters. "No. I mean, yes. The band is great. I was just being stupid. I'm sorry."

Xander laughs. "She's just kidding, Luke. She's not in the band."

Lucas shakes his head and meets my eyes in the

rearview mirror. "You said it with such a straight face I thought for sure you were serious."

"She's really good at sarcasm."

I tap the back of Xander's headrest. "I thought we agreed on the word 'exceptionally.'"

"I'm trying not to encourage you."

"And does it work?"

Lucas smiles. "Maybe the benefit won't be as boring as I thought. She's sitting at our table, right?"

"Caymen is smart. She refuses to go with me."

"What?" Lucas punches Xander in the arm. "Has that ever happened before? Do I need to write this down somewhere?" He looks around and then ends up grabbing his phone from the center console and holding it to his mouth like a recording device. "A girl refused to go somewhere with Xander. Alert the media."

"Whatever," Xander says.

"And while we're on the topic. Two weeks in a row? Pretty impressive, bro. I must be too boring for them to care about these days."

"What are you talking about?" Xander asks.

"*Starz.*" He rolls his eyes with a sigh when Xander looks oblivious. If I didn't know exactly what Lucas was talking about I might look oblivious, too. "The magazine. You. Front page."

"Seriously?" He sounds more angry than surprised.

"Yes. They have you dating Sadie again."

"What?" He points past the light where we're stopped and to the Quickie Mart on the opposite corner. "Stop there."

Lucas shrugs and obeys the directions, parking the car. Xander barely waits for it to stop moving before he jumps out and disappears into the glowing store.

CHAPTER 29

. . . .

While we wait in the car Lucas turns all the way around in his seat, resting his arm across the back. "What's that about?"

My heart is racing. The girlfriend "secret" is out, and I wonder what Xander is going to say or do now. "He must be mad that they printed something about him and Sadie."

"You're probably right. I just thought he knew."

"Me, too."

Minutes later a *Starz* magazine is slapped against the window next to me, making me jump in surprise.

"You read this?" he yells through the window. I can barely hear him.

He opens the door and climbs in next to me without waiting for me to scoot over. "You read this, didn't you?"

He's practically on top of me. I slide down the seat to make room for him.

"Drive, Lucas," he says, pulling the door shut. Then his eyes are back on me and there's fire in them.

"Are you mad at me for reading an article? Mason showed it to me last week."

"Last week! Caymen, why didn't you say something?"

"What did you want me to say? 'Wow, your girlfriend is hot?' Wasn't feeling that generous."

Lucas laughs and Xander shoots him a look that shuts him up.

"That's the point, though. She's not my girlfriend."

"But the article . . ." I point to the magazine he's clutching in his fist.

"This"—he flicks the face of Sadie on the front of the magazine— "is an old picture." He studies it closer. "Last year."

"And she called you the other day. . . ."

"She called me? No, she didn't."

"I may have answered it. . . . She said she'd call back."

He pulls out his phone and scrolls through some screens. Then he grunts as if to say, *Oh look, there she is.*

He presses the speaker button on his phone and a message left by Sadie Newel broadcasts in the car. "Hey, Xander. Where are you? Did you see *Starz* magazine? Those idiots. What's the plan? I need you to work your magic to make that disappear. Tell me your father will hit them hard." She sounds irritated.

Xander hangs up then slowly turns his gaze to me, one eyebrow raised.

"Oh" is all I can think of to say.

"Oh?"

"What do you expect me to say? I saw an article. I knew you were in LA that weekend. I'm sorry I thought all journalists were honest."

"What I expect," he says, leaning close, "is for you to ask me." His eyes are so intense I want to look away . . . or never look away, I can't decide.

My heart is pumping fast, and I'm so relieved that he is not with Sadie Newel that I almost throw my arms around him. Joke. I need a joke. Fast. "Maybe you should give me a list of all the actresses you've dated and in what year. That way I'll know if it's an old picture or a new one."

"I can get you that list," Lucas says.

I drag my eyes away from Xander and on to Lucas. "Could you include any heiresses or billionaires' daughters as well? Anyone newsworthy, really."

"It might take me a while. That's an extensive list."

I know he's joking with me, but the words hit home, reminding me that I wouldn't come close to making that list.

Xander sighs and leans back. "It's not that long." He puts his hand over mine on the seat between us. I try not to smile too big.

We pull up to the redbrick buildings of an expansive campus and I'm confused. "Where are we?"

"UNLV."

"Is this your pitch for college?"

"No. You'll see." It's so funny how excited Xander gets to take me on these career days. Maybe Xander should be a life planner or something. Does that career exist?

It takes me the whole walk through the sprawling campus to realize something. "You go to school here," I say to Lucas.

"Yes, I do."

It surprises me. Not that UNLV is a bad school. I just thought he would be at an Ivy League. I still haven't figured out why we're here, though.

After passing a lot of buildings that look similar to one another, we finally enter one. At the end of the hall he knocks on a door. A man with glasses answers with a smile. "Hello. Come in."

I take in the room. Microscopes, burners, vials, glass

cases, petri dishes. The science department. The man—a TA maybe?—says, "I hear you might be interested in studying science."

My lungs feel close to bursting. "Yes."

He goes on about all the different careers a degree in science can lead to. Medical, crime-scene investigation, research analysis, and on and on. Almost every one he mentions sounds interesting to me.

"Follow me," he says, and leads me to a microscope. "I was just getting ready to analyze this blood sample. What I'm looking for is to see how many white blood cells per square unit there are. If you'll just look through the scope and count for me I'll see if my number matches yours."

I do as he asked and relay my number. He writes it in a box on the paper next to the microscope. Then he goes to a glass case and pulls out a vial. He lets me inject a needle into it and drop a different drop of blood onto a slide and analyze that one as well. Next he shows me some different bacteria they were growing in dishes and tells me what each was taken from and the results. He also shows me some old police files that the students were working on to assess DNA and cause of death.

I know I must have an awestruck look on my face because when I glance over at Xander he has the biggest smile I have ever seen.

"Are you majoring in science, Lucas?" I ask.

"No. I'm an architecture major. This is just one of my classes. And Rick here is my roommate. He's the TA for Dr. Fenderman."

"Has Dr. Fenderman lured us here for future use as test subjects?"

"Yes, the next stop on the tour is the cage."

"Cool. Does he happen to be testing any vaccinations? These boys need to catch some debilitating illness to get out of going to a benefit."

"My sympathies," Rick says. Has everyone in the world gone to a benefit besides me? Rick clips another slide in place and I peer through the microscope. Lucas and Rick start talking, and as I'm studying the slide I feel a tickle on the back of my neck.

"Are you having fun yet?" Xander asks. I feel him now, close behind me, the heat from his body sending a chill up my spine.

"Yes. This is amazing."

"I've never seen you so happy."

I've never felt so happy. I'm still looking through the lens at the slide, but I'm not seeing anything because Xander's breath lightly touches the back of my neck. My body reacts to him, almost involuntarily, leaning back against his chest.

He wraps his arms around my shoulders. "You should major in science. Not necessarily here, but the field suits you. I could see you looking all cute in a white lab coat."

I smile. "It's a good idea. Maybe in a year." I'm definitely taking at least a year off to help my mom.

"Caymen." His voice is disapproving, like he knows what I am thinking. "That's a mistake."

"Yeah, well, I don't have many options, Xander."

"You have as many options as you give yourself."

I laugh a little. *He* has as many options as he gives himself. The rest of us are stuck with what's given to us. "Why do you care?" I whisper.

For a second I think he didn't hear me because I'm facing away from him, his arms still wrapped around my shoulders, but then he says, "Because I care about you." I close my eyes for one second and let myself feel those words, feel him.

I want to let this happen, but something is still holding me back. I thought it was his girlfriend. But that's obviously not an issue anymore. It's my mother. I haven't told her. And I feel terrible for that. I didn't want to be his dirty little secret, but I have made him mine. I'm glad my back is to him because I can feel the disgust for myself written all over my face. I wiggle my arms, forcing him to drop his, and look at the clock on the wall. "Is it really eight already? We better go, Xander."

"Before we leave, there's this little Mexican joint on The Strip that I have to take you to. It's not far. Amazing food."

CHAPTER 30

• • • • • • •

"So he took you on a plane and *flew* you to a science department to give you a taste of college life and your rebuttal is . . . ?" Skye is trying to make me do something over the top for our next career day, but how am I supposed to top that?

"Um, actually, he's coming over tomorrow night because my mom has this business associations meeting. . . ." I don't know how to finish that thought and grab a small jewelry box off a shelf. It has fake jewels glued all over the wooden lid and is a perfect example of why I call this place Obvious Garbage.

Skye is busy arranging old books on a shelf, her back to me. "I don't get it. How is that a career day? Are you going to take him to the meeting? Let him see how small business owners argue?"

"No." I put the jewelry box down. "No, actually, I think my mom isn't going to the meeting. I think she's going out with some guy. A behind-my-back date."

She turns around now, hands on her hips. "Wait. Are you saying that you and your mom are both dating people behind each other's backs?" She laughs.

"No. I'm not dating Xander." Yet. Not until I work up the courage to tell my mom. I've given myself one week to do that.

She rolls her eyes. "You two are the most in-love not-dating people I've met. Hold on." She walks toward the back of the store and calls to Lydia, the owner. "The books are in order and the sign is flipped. Do you need me to do anything else?"

"No. Have a good night. I'll see you tomorrow."

Skye hooks her arm around my elbow and leads me out the back door, cutting across the alley to the back of the doll store. "Where's your mom?" she asks, pointing to the empty space where our car is normally parked.

"She ran to the store after we closed."

"So anyway, back to career day. I don't get what you're going to do with Xander."

"Neither do I. I was planning on spying on my mom. But I can see it's a bad idea."

She laughs.

"I had one other idea for a career day."

We walk up the stairs to my apartment.

"I talked to Eddie last week and he said he'd teach us how to make his famous muffins."

Skye makes a face. "Why?"

"Because Xander likes them. He likes all food, really. Everywhere we go we end up at his favorite restaurant. I thought maybe he could talk to Eddie, see if owning his own restaurant is something he'd enjoy."

"Aww," Skye says. "Now that's thoughtful. And sweet." She walks to the fridge once we're inside. "And you pretend not to love the guy."

I smile as she digs through the contents of the fridge. The light on the answering machine is blinking. I hit the button. "One new message," the robotic voice says, followed by a lady. "Hi, Ms. Meyers, this is Tina from Dr. Saunders's office. We went ahead and scheduled that ultrasound for you on the fifteenth. Please show up half an hour early and make sure you drink all the water we talked about. If you have any questions please don't hesitate to call."

I hear the fridge close behind me.

"I didn't know your mom was pregnant," Skye says.

"Pregnant? What?"

"Ultrasound. That's what they do for pregnant people."

My brain is just barely registering the words she said. "No, she's not."

"Oh, then why is she getting an ultrasound?"

There have to be other reasons people get ultrasounds. "I don't know."

"Has she been nauseous? Tired?"

I think back. She hadn't been eating very well lately. Maybe it's because she's been sick to her stomach. And she has definitely been tired. I nod.

"So she's probably pregnant." She nods her head toward the answering machine. "Plus they asked her to drink all that water. That's what they tell pregnant people to do so they can get measurements."

I shake my head back and forth over and over.

"It's kind of exciting, though, don't you think? You're going to have a little brother or sister."

"Exciting? Yeah, right. No. She's not pregnant. That's ridiculous. She doesn't even have a . . ." I realize I was about to say "boyfriend." It's very possible that she does have a boyfriend. "She's not pregnant." But if she's not pregnant then what is she? Anxiety washes over me. Is something wrong with her? People don't get ultrasounds just because. . . . Do they? Maybe once you're older that's a standard procedure.

Skye moves in front of me and pets my shoulders. I must've gone completely catatonic. "It's probably not a big deal. Even if she is pregnant it's not a big deal."

"She's not pregnant," I insist. "She's too old to be pregnant."

Skye laughs. "She's only thirty-five." Her phone chimes and she pulls it out and smiles after reading the text. "It's Henry. The band is hanging out at Scream Shout. You want to go?"

I look at the now-solid light on the answering machine. Then I glance at the door. I can't catch my breath. When will my mom be home? I need to ask her about this. But will she tell me? She's been refusing to tell me anything for weeks now.

It's nothing. My mom is fine. Standard procedure. "Yes. I'll be right down. Give me one minute."

She hesitates but then leaves. I scribble a note about spending the night at Skye's and leave it on the counter. I pack a few things in my backpack and lock the door behind me.

We walk into Scream Shout and it's practically deserted. The bartender points to the door off to the side of the stage when Skye gives him the questioning shoulder raise. Then she marches across the club and straight to the door. Music from a back room seeps down the dim hall. We follow the sound. The band is sitting on couches in a small back room and look up when we enter.

Henry greets Skye by singing a soft "There's my beautiful girl," accompanied by a few strums of his guitar.

She smiles and slides into the small space between him and the arm of the couch.

Mason winks at me. "Hey, Caymen."

"Hi." I throw my backpack against the wall, find some floor space, and settle in. I just want to melt into the floor and fade from existence for a while. It seems to work as the guys start goofing around with lyrics and music. I let the blended melodies bounce around inside me.

Derrick, the drummer, randomly sings about his day. How he drove in his car and listened to the radio. How he went to the store and picked up some milk and on and on. I stop listening until he asks, "What rhymes with 'fire hydrant'?"

Mason gets serious and I think he's going to say something like "Don't be an idiot. Why are you singing about a fire hydrant?" But instead he says, "I don't know, 'wire tyrant'?"

"What's a wire tyrant?" Henry asks.

"You know, someone who hoards all the wire. It's a rising epidemic."

I give a small laugh.

"How about 'tired rant'?" Skye says. "If you draw it out, it rhymes good enough."

"This is our tired rant about a useless fire hydrant," Henry sings.

Mason laughs. "This is our tired rant about Henry the wire tyrant."

"How can a rant be tired?" I ask. "Aren't rants by nature lively?"

Henry strums a chord, looks up at the ceiling for a minute while playing several more chords, then sings, "I'm so tired of the same old rant when what I really need is a second chance."

Mason points at him. "Yes. Let's call this song 'Fire Hydrant.'"

They laugh, but Derrick starts writing on a notepad as they yell out more lines about making up and starting over. I don't believe I just witnessed the birth of a song that started out with the words "fire hydrant." It's weird to see something created from nothing. I think about myself and how Xander is trying to create something out of my nothing life. How he kind of has. He took the ridiculousness, the fire hydrant, from my song and made me realize it could be something more, something different.

After the day I had, this thought makes me happy.

I start shouting out lines with them. They get pretty far on the song before ridiculousness is reintroduced when someone yells, "And why won't you just let me eat turtle soup?"

Skye gasps in offense but then everyone laughs.

At ten o'clock the laughter has not ceased. We've gotten past laughter and into slaphappy stupidity. Skye is on the floor draped across me. "I better get you home, little girl," she says. "It's a school night for the under-age one."

"I'm spending the night at your house!" I yell.

"You are?"

"That's what my note told me so it must be true."

"Yay! Slumber party."

"We should toilet paper someone's house," I say.

"Yes. We should TP someone's house. Whose?"

"I don't know." Then I raise my hand like she's a teacher. "Xander's!"

She laughs. "Who wants to TP Xander's house?"

The guys just look at us and groan.

"We don't need you." I stand. "Let's go."

Skye runs ahead, but just as I clear the door, I'm tugged back by my arm. I whirl around and face-plant against Mason's chest. We're standing just outside the door in the dim corridor.

He kisses my cheek. "You left without saying good-bye."

I step back and meet his eyes. "I'm . . ."

He blinks hard. "You and Xander, huh?"

"I think so."

"Are you sure you fit?"

I know exactly what he means, but as an image of Xander pops into my head I nod.

He shrugs a lazy shrug. "You know where to find me." With that he disappears back into the room.

CHAPTER 31

Skye and I each hold two rolls of toilet paper and stare at the gated fence of Xander's house. "Isn't it too early to TP?" Skye asks. "It's not even ten thirty. The house lights are all on."

"It's never too early. The real question is how are we going to get inside?" I try to squeeze through two wrought iron bars and my thigh gets stuck. I start laughing.

"Have you ever been this irresponsible in your life?" Skye asks.

"I don't think so."

"The silly you is fun." Skye takes me by the armpits and tries to pull me out. She's a laughing mess. Finally she tugs me free and I land on top of her, both of us falling to the ground.

"Let's just TP the bars of the gate."

"Is Xander going to find this as funny as we do?" she asks.

I have no idea. "For sure."

It's dark, but we manage to wrap toilet paper around the bars. When did being immature provide so much entertainment? It takes me a minute to realize I can see my task better and another minute to realize it's because someone is shining a flashlight. The flashlight holder clears his throat. "Ladies. You enjoying yourselves?"

"Yes, very much," Skye says, and we both turn around to a security personnel of sorts giving us a disapproving stare.

"How cute. It's a rent-a-cop," Skye says.

He lowers his brows. "A rent-a-cop who knows the number for the police station. Let's go have a word with Mr. Spence, shall we?"

This news should've introduced some somberness into the evening but it doesn't. Maybe because it didn't seem real when we were standing there holding toilet paper in the dark. It seems a lot more real standing on Mr. Spence's porch with him scrutinizing us. Then how come I still can't stop laughing?

"What would you like me to do, sir?" Rent-a-cop asks.

Mr. Spence looks at me again and tilts his head. I wonder if he'll remember having met me before. Why would he? I'm just a name he met weeks ago. So when he says, "Caymen? Right?" the smile is shocked from my face.

I nod. Of course he remembers me. I am the symbol of his son's rebellion. I am the last girl on earth Mr. Spence would approve of. My name and face are probably ingrained in his memory.

"Are you pranking my son?"

I nod again.

He laughs. "I'll be honest. None of my kids have ever been toilet-papered. Is that what it's called?" He turns to the rent-a-cop. "We're fine, Bruce." Then back to us he says, "Why don't you girls come in?"

My chest tightens in panic as I look at the toilet paper rolls still gripped in my hands. "No. That's okay. We'll go now. If you loan me a trash bag we'll even clean up the mess."

He waves off the suggestion. "No. We have groundskeepers for that. And I insist. You must come inside."

"It's late. We—"

"Caymen?"

Xander's voice is like an instant heat wave. My cheeks go warm. He comes to the door wearing pajama bottoms and a T-shirt. Even his pajamas look expensive. He looks at the toilet paper in my hands and then over to Skye and her toilet paper.

"It was a dare," I blurt out. "We weren't supposed to get caught." Skye starts to giggle and I join her.

His eyes twinkle with a held-in laugh. "Come in. Tess made hot chocolate earlier. I think there's some left."

I'm not sure if I'm supposed to know who Tess is but I don't ask. Holding toilet paper is enough humiliation for one night. "No, thanks. Really, we were just leaving."

"I insist," he says.

Skye gives a snort laugh and I'm pretty sure it's because Xander just sounded exactly like his dad. I can tell she's holding her tongue to let me decide how this is going to play out. I look between Xander and his father, who are both staring at me expectantly with the same crossed arms, the same tilt to their brows. Seeing such an obvious resemblance makes me wonder if I'm anything like my dad. I may look like my mom, but I'm nothing like her.

"Fine. Just for a minute. It's late. We honestly didn't mean to intrude."

The kitchen is huge. Marble countertops in a neutral shade. A massive island. The fridge is bigger than any fridge I've ever seen in a house. It almost looks like a grocery store freezer section.

His dad follows us into the kitchen. "Tess has actually left for the night, but I'm sure you kids can find your way around."

Tess must be the cook.

"Good night. Alexander, don't make it too late," he says, then leaves.

Xander goes to the stove, where a kettle sits, and picks it up. "Empty."

"We're fine."

"No, I got this. I think there is the powder stuff somewhere around here." He looks through cupboards. He's obviously not going to stop until we are drinking hot chocolate, so I go to the stove and grab the kettle, fill it with water, and then stare at the knobs. Skye comes over to help me decipher them. After turning several and pushing a few buttons, we get one of the burners' flames on.

Xander is still searching for the hot chocolate. He looks like a stranger in his own kitchen, opening doors he obviously has no clue what's behind. Finally he snatches the container out from behind a cupboard with a loud "Aha."

"Have you ever looked inside these cupboards in your life?" I ask.

"Of course."

"Let's play a game, then. Skye names a kitchen item. Whoever finds it first wins."

"Wins what?"

"Bragging rights."

"This is my house. I think I'll win."

"Prove it, rich boy. Tess isn't here to make your bottle for you."

"Oh, you are so on."

I smile. I know my way around a kitchen. And if a cook set it up she would be smart and practical. Cooking utensils by the stove, glasses by the sink. I have this. I nod to Skye.

She smiles. "Okay. We'll start easy. Spatula."

Xander runs to the island and starts tearing through the drawers. I go to the stove and pull open the drawers on either side of it. Right away I find the spatula and turn around holding it up.

"First round to Caymen," Skye says, and Xander snaps his head up to look at me. He growls.

"Okay, second item. Cereal bowl."

I give a grunt of indignation. "So not fair. You knew he'd know where that is." And of course he does. Cupboard beside the pantry.

"Tiebreaker," Skye calls out. "Find me a strainer."

I laugh at the look on Xander's face. It's a look that says, *I don't even know what that is.* I race toward the sink.

It will be underneath one of the cupboards there. When I reach for the cupboard a pair of hands grab my waist and pull me back. Then he cuts around me and yanks open the cupboard I was going for. I jolt forward and settle in next to him, trying to push him aside with my body.

"Cheater," he says.

"Me? You're the cheater." He's standing firm. I can't push him over and he's searching the shelves.

"It's like a bowl with holes in it," Skye calls out.

"My own best friend is against me." I wrap my arms around Xander's waist and try to pull him back. The kettle on the stove whistles and Skye removes it from the burner.

"Got it!" Xander holds the strainer in the air. I jump up and try to grab it and he keeps it just out of my reach. When I try to pull his arm down, he puts his free arm around my shoulder, pinning me against his chest. "And the winner is Xander."

"Cheaters! The both of you!"

He clears his throat. "I'd like to dedicate this win to my supreme knowledge of the kitchen layout and tools therein that I have used on many occasions. If it wasn't for—" He stops mid-sentence and then says, "Oh, hi, Mom."

I immediately drop my hands that are pushing against

Xander's chest and try to twist out of his hold. He sets the strainer on the counter and secures me with both arms. "Mom, this is Caymen Meyers and her friend Skye."

I turn my head toward her because my body is still trapped in Xander's grip. I'm afraid of what I'll see on her face. Afraid this will be the moment when I finally meet the resistance to this relationship on his end. But she has a pleasant look on her way-too-young-to-be-Xander's-mother face. Her hair is blond. Her eyes are blue. Now I see where Lucas gets his looks from. Xander didn't inherit a thing from his mother. But then she smiles, perhaps because I start struggling against Xander, and I see that he inherited his best feature from her.

"Good to meet you, girls. Caymen, I've heard so much about you."

"Hello, Mrs. Spence. Your son won't let me go because he's a cheater, but it's good to meet you."

Xander releases me, and I back away from him a few steps, trying to keep my explosion of giddiness to myself.

Mrs. Spence picks up a roll of toilet paper from the counter and scrunches her nose.

"Ask Caymen about that," Xander says.

Great, now I have to explain to his mother about my vandalism? "Your son called me with a toilet paper emergency. I rushed right over."

She looks confused so Xander says, "She's kidding, Mom."

"Ah, yes. The dry humor you were telling me about."

Jeez, how much did they talk about me?

"Well, I'm glad you've gotten my serious boy laughing." She squeezes my arm and then pats Xander's cheek. "I'm off to bed. Don't be a stranger, Caymen."

"Night, Mom." After his mom leaves, Xander moves to the mugs and scoops a few spoonfuls of powdered chocolate into each then pours the hot water. "This isn't as good as Eddie's but I hope it'll do."

"Do you have a bathroom somewhere?" Skye asks. "Or ten?"

He smiles. "The closest one is through that arch. First door on your right."

"Thanks."

She leaves and it's just Xander and me standing side by side at the counter. His hip presses against my side as he reaches for a spoon. Then our hands brush as we reach for the same mug. We both pull back from it.

"Go ahead," we say at the same time and then laugh. He takes a sip of the hot chocolate and then slides the mug to me.

The entire sides of our bodies are touching—shoulders, elbows, hips, thighs—all the way down to our feet. I can feel every tiny movement he makes.

"You're killing me," he says breathlessly.

"I'm sorry." I take one step away, and he grabs me by the elbow and swings me to face him. Now the entire fronts of our bodies are touching. I take a sharp breath as heat pours down me. He backs me up against the counter. His palm pressing into my lower back feels like it could singe a handprint onto my skin.

I'm staring as hard as I can at the collar of his T-shirt.

"Caymen?"

"Yes?"

"You look terrified. Does this scare you?"

"More than anything."

"Why?"

"Because I didn't bring my mints."

"And now the real answer . . ."

"Because I'm afraid that once you catch me, the game's over." I don't believe I admitted that out loud to him when I hadn't even admitted it to myself. But he called me out. He always calls me out.

His finger traces my cheekbone and my heart slams into my rib cage as the nerves from my cheek all the way down my arms buzz to life.

"I didn't realize we were playing a game," he says.

I smile. That was the same line he had used during our second meeting. I look at him, and as if that's all he'd been waiting for, his lips meet mine. When they touch I feel electrified. He kisses me gently, his lips as warm as his hand.

Just when I'm about to go into attack mode, I hear Skye clear her throat and say, "I'm just going to take my hot chocolate to go, then. I'll bring your mug back another time."

I pull back and try to push Xander away, not wanting to be rude, but he doesn't budge. Skye gives me the *way to go* smile and I realize she's not offended at all.

"I'll give her a ride home," Xander says without looking away from me. His eyes are on fire. We both listen as Skye leaves the kitchen. Then he takes me by the waist and lifts me onto the counter. I wrap my legs and arms around him and press my lips to his. The action is more intense this time. My need more obvious.

He answers back, his tongue finding mine, his hands pulling me as close as possible. He tastes good, like salty chocolate. I let my hands explore his back through his T-shirt. I find his spine and outline each vertebra. A rush of emotions courses through my body, and I'm surprised when the one that overwhelms me is intense sadness, the one emotion I've been successfully repressing all night.

I am moments away from tears so I bury my head in his neck, hoping to suppress them. He freezes. He tries to back up, probably so he can look at me, but I cling tightly to him. He rubs a hand up and down my back.

"Caymen? What is it? I'm sorry. Was that too fast?" He takes me by the waist and slides me off the counter.

"No. It's not that."

"I'm so sorry."

"No, you didn't do anything. This is really bad timing

for my denial to lift." I'm not sure if he understood what I said because my emotions are making my speech thick.

"Talk to me. What happened?"

"Will you just hold me for a minute?" I'm trying to get my emotions in check before I try to explain.

He must realize he had dropped his hands to his sides because he takes a deep breath and then wraps them back around me. There is not a millimeter of space between us. His presence is the only thing keeping me together while the thoughts I should've been thinking all night finally surface.

What if my mom is pregnant? Having a baby is going to ruin us. We can't afford it. And what kind of guy is Matthew? Is he going to run when he finds out? How can my mom have made the same mistake twice? If I thought I had a tiny bit of hope of leaving the doll store and starting a life of my own, this would make that almost impossible.

A single tear escapes and I swipe it away quickly with the back of my hand.

"You're scaring me, Caymen. What is it?"

"My mom."

"Is she okay?" He sounds alarmed.

"She might be pregnant."

CHAPTER 32

• • • • • • •

Xander curses under his breath. "Man, Caymen, I'm sorry." That's all he says for a while. His fingers create a trail on my back: across, down, over, up. They repeat the pattern over and over. "When did you find out?"

"Tonight." I sigh. "Or maybe she's not. And I'm wishing so bad she's not. But if she isn't that means something else is wrong with her and that I'm a horrible daughter for thinking even for a split second that I'd rather her be anything but pregnant."

He pushes me out by the shoulders and I let him. When we meet eyes he says, "What can I do?"

"Make this all a dream that I can wake up from tomorrow."

He pulls on his bottom lip. "I feel like I took advantage of you tonight. I'm sorry. Had I known I would have never—"

"Stop," I interrupt. "Don't say that. I've been wanting to kiss you for weeks. Way before I found out about my mom, back when you used to walk me to school."

His eyes flicker to my lips then back to my eyes. "You wanted to kiss me?"

"'Want' is the correct word. I *want* to kiss you." I lean forward and brush my lips against his.

He pulls back a little. "Now I'd really be a jerk if we kissed. Come on. Let's talk." He leads me down the hall by my hand to a large theater room. Several overstuffed recliners set on different levels face a big white screen.

"Wow," I say, spinning in a circle. "This is where we need to watch *The Shining*."

He lifts one side of his mouth into a half-smile then goes to a bookshelf full of DVDs and pulls out the one with Jack Nicholson sticking his creepy face through a gap in a door.

"You got it?"

"I did. You said we were going to watch it so I got it."

I plop down in a recliner. "Well, put it on, then."

He shakes his head. "Not tonight. Tonight we talk."

He replaces the movie and settles into the recliner next to mine.

"What were you doing before I got here?"

"Let me rephrase that: tonight we talk about *you*."

"Can we just work up to it first? I'm not good at things like this."

He nods. "Okay, before you got here? Let's see, I was working on a history assignment."

"Do you go to Dalton Academy or Oceanside?" They're both private schools. I'm sure he goes to one or the other.

"Dalton."

"Dalton . . . that's your grandma's last name." Before I even finish the sentence I feel stupid for saying it. "Duh. That's not a coincidence."

He laughs. "Thanks, by the way."

"For what?"

"For reminding me what it's like to be treated like a normal person. It's been a long time since I've been around someone who didn't know who I was."

I tilt my head. "Wait, who are you?"

He tugs on my hair with a smirk.

"Your parents are really nice."

"When they get what they want, yes they are."

"So have you been working on the website for your dad, then?"

He draws out a sigh. "That's the thing. I have. I know, I know, I shouldn't."

I hold up my hands. "I said nothing."

"So I had all these great ideas for the website to make it fresh and exciting and my dad completely disregarded all of them. He said, 'No, clean and classic.'"

"For your clientele that's probably better."

"What do you mean?"

"I mean it's not like teenagers are going to book rooms at your hotels. It's businessmen and wealthy people. Clean and classic work for them."

He closes his eyes for a second then says, "You're right. Why didn't he just say that?"

"Maybe he tried. You don't listen to your dad very well."

"Because he wants to shape me into this perfect little version of him and I feel smothered. I'm not him."

"Isn't it funny that you want to be nothing like your dad and I wish I knew if I am even a tiny bit like mine?"

"I'm sorry. I'm being insensitive."

I touch his shoulder. "No, you're not. I get what you're saying. You don't want to be defined by your father. Especially when from the outside you are so similar to him. But you aren't him. You'll always be different." *You'll always be amazing.* Why is it still so hard to say that last sentence out loud?

He takes my hand in his and runs his thumb along the

back of it. "Your father would be so proud of you. Of who you are."

My entire throat closes with the comment and my eyes fill with tears. I keep them at bay but am surprised by the strong reaction. By how much I needed to hear someone say that. "He lives in New York. He's some fancy lawyer there."

"You've looked him up?"

"I had to. I might need a kidney one day."

He laughs.

"When I was twelve I read this story about some guy who hadn't seen his father in years and then he ended up getting cancer. His father was a bone marrow match. Saved his life."

Xander stares at me for so long I start to feel uncomfortable. "You don't have to be on your deathbed to reach out to your father, you know."

I rub at my forearm. "He walked away from my mom."

He nods slowly. "You feel like wanting to see him means betraying your mother?"

I look up at the light but another tear escapes anyway. "He left her."

"Her relationship with him doesn't have to define yours."

"He left me, too."

"I'm sorry." He runs the back of his knuckles along

my cheek. "And what about your mom? Why is her possible pregnancy so devastating?"

"You think I'm overreacting?"

"I did not say that at all. I know I'd be upset if it were my mom. I just don't want to project my reasons onto you. Tell me what's going through your head."

"I'm angry and hurt and ashamed all wrapped together into one emotional mess. I just don't believe she would do this again." I pull my knees up onto the chair and turn sideways to face him. "I feel guilty and selfish for wishing a person out of existence but I don't want this change."

"You'll work through those feelings. You'll melt when you hold the baby in your arms."

"No, I won't. I don't like kids and kids don't like me. We've come to this general consensus long ago."

He smiles. "Well, at least you have a long time to get used to the idea."

"If it's true." I sigh and squeeze my eyes closed.

His thumb makes small circles on the back of my hand. "It's so nice to have you here. In my house. You should come here every day."

I laugh. "I'm best in small doses. Speaking of, I should probably get going. We have school tomorrow."

"No way. You have to stay at least another hour." He pulls me into the chair with him. "Thanks for talking to me. I know it's hard for you."

I rest my forehead against his. "Thanks for listening."

"We still on for tomorrow night?"

Tomorrow night? Oh! Career night. My mom supposedly going to the business association meeting. There is no way I'm going to miss that now. "We're still on."

"And what about tonight?" he asks, wrapping his arms tightly around me.

My stomach seems to take flight without me. "What about tonight?"

"What should we do for the next hour?"

I pretend to consider. "Work on your website?"

"Ha-ha."

I make my face serious, which is hard considering the smile that wants to take up permanent residence there. "No, really, you should get it done."

He tilts his head, studying my face. "Are you being serious?"

"No," I say against his lips.

CHAPTER 33

• • • • • • •

I open the shop door while holding the bell steady and yank Xander inside.

"What the—?"

"Shh." I listen for several heartbeats to make sure my mom didn't come back inside through the back door. She had just left . . . late. I had told Xander to come at six thirty, a whole half an hour after she was supposed to leave, but as the minutes ticked by I realized it would be a close call. It actually worked out better this way because now we can follow her. Before, I was just thinking we'd have to find her.

242

When I finally take a breath and look up at Xander, he's staring at me in the dark room. I have one hand on his chest and have him pushed up against the wall just inside the store. My breath falters.

His breath shouldn't smell so familiar already. I let it wash over me, closing my eyes. Then I feel his lips brush against mine. I want to get lost in his kiss but I know we don't have time.

"Come on." I grab on to the front of his shirt, pull him to the back door, then open it a crack. Luigi's is one block behind us, and I see my mom round the corner at the end of the alley.

"Caymen," Xander says from behind me. "Can you fill me in here?"

"A little detective work. Private investigators or something." I reach into my back pocket and pull out the few pictures I had taken of Matthew with Xander's camera. I'd printed them out. The quality is really bad since our printer is ancient, but the image is clear enough.

"What am I looking at?"

I slip outside and he follows. "I need to find out everything there is to know about that guy."

"Okay . . . what do we know so far?"

"Nothing."

He clears his throat. "Miss Scientific Observer has no concrete facts?"

"I have a feeling." That if my mom is pregnant I need to know everything I can about the potential father.

"Do feelings prove theories now?"

"Shut up."

He laughs and grabs hold of my hand. It surprises me and I must jump because he squeezes it with a chuckle. It's weird holding his hand. I think about the picture I saw in the magazine of him and Sadie holding hands and wonder if someone is waiting in the shadows now to take a picture of us.

Almost as if he read my mind he says, "We moved here to get out of the spotlight. Los Angeles is awful. We had no privacy there whatsoever."

I nod, not sure what the proper response to that is.

"But considering this isn't exactly the thriving metropolis of California and how spread out our business is, we travel a lot. My father drags me along on some occasions. Like tomorrow. I have to go to Florida until Friday and then I have the benefit on Saturday."

He's not asking my permission . . . is he? He's just telling me because . . . because why? We're together now?

"I guess my point is when can I see you again?"

"Oh. Next week?"

"You'll pencil me in on the really big calendar?"

"I don't know. It might be booked solid. My super busy life and I will have to check."

When we round the corner I can see the red and white awning of Luigi's Italian Restaurant . . . and the back of my mom as she closes the door behind her. Hmm. That's not what was supposed to happen. She was supposed to meet up with tall, dark, and creepy.

"What now?" Xander asks.

"We wait." I walk to a small patch of grass on the corner of the block that gives us a good view of Luigi's but isn't in full view of the window. I sit down. "Worried about ruining your jeans?" I ask when he hesitates. "It's not wet."

"No . . . it's just . . . are we spying on your mom?" He sits down next to me.

"Yes," I admit with a wince.

"Caymen, I know you're upset, but is this really the right way to go about it?"

I point to the pictures he's still holding. "I need to know about him."

He flips through the pictures again. "Is this him? The father of . . ." He can't even finish the sentence. It's like he's as ashamed as I am. I wonder if he's ever known anyone who got pregnant out of wedlock.

"Yes." I lean back on my palms.

He nods once then looks around. "So how long are we going to wait here?"

I glance toward Luigi's. "I don't know." Maybe she's

going to see Matthew after the meeting. I take the pictures he's still holding back and look through them again.

"So you think I'd make a good detective?"

"What?"

"Tonight. Your 'career night.'" He actually does air quotes and manages to make them look somewhat classy. "That's what you said tonight was, right? You're supposed to be finding me suitable options to explore. Is detective work something you think I'd be good at?"

"Yeah. Sure."

"Because I'm so good at observations and reading into clues and interpreting signals?" He picks at the grass, pulling a few blades free. He looks so hurt.

My warning light goes off, telling me to back up, fix this; tell him, "No, it was about me and my mom and I just needed your help." I open my mouth, but it's too late.

He stands up and brushes off his hands then holds one out to me. "I'll walk you back."

"I'm staying."

"Okay." He starts to walk away.

"I'm sorry," I say to his back. He stops. "I've been so self-absorbed and lame. You've done all these amazing things for me and I haven't done anything for you. I took you grave digging. You took me to UNLV."

He turns to face me.

I point up the street. "I was going to take you to Eddie's. He was going to teach us how to make his famous muffins and tell us how he started his business and stuff. I thought you might like it because you love food and I could see you owning your own restaurant or something. But then this happened and . . ."

He closes the distance between us, takes my face in his hands, and kisses me.

I can't breathe for a moment, and then all I want to do is breathe him in. Eat, sleep, and drink Xander Spence. I can't get enough. I don't know how I existed without him because his energy feels like my sustaining force in this moment.

He pulls away a little and I take a gulp of air. I lie back on the grass because my bones can no longer hold me up. He lies sideways next to me, propping himself up on his elbow.

"I bought a dress," I say in my state of bliss.

"Um . . . how exciting."

"If you want me to I can go to the benefit with you on Saturday."

"If?" He shakes his head. "I would love for you to come to the benefit. I just thought you were dead set against it. Yes. Come." He kisses me again and I laugh against his lips. I bury my fingers in the hair at the back of his neck. He squeezes my side and I laugh again.

I didn't hear any footsteps or the jingling of keys. All I hear is someone clear their throat. I sit up too fast and blood rushes up the back of my head, causing the edges of my vision to blur for a moment. But blurry or not, I can still see my mom's face staring down at us, filled with anger.

CHAPTER 34

For some reason I giggle. Maybe because I still can't control the happy pounding of my heart. Maybe because I'm still so angry with my mom for all the secrets she's been keeping that seeing her angry with me brings some satisfaction. Or maybe because I have absolutely no idea what to say. Whatever the case, a giggle sounds funny in the otherwise still night. "Hi."

She looks at Xander, starting at his freshly cut hair and ending on his expensive shoes. Then her contemptuous look is back on me. "I'll see you at home." And with that she walks away. I suck in my lips to stop myself from laughing. When she rounds the corner I lie back and pull Xander down with me. I kiss him but he resists.

"Caymen, wait."

"What?"

"She doesn't know about us?"

"You knew that."

"No. I didn't. I thought after I introduced myself to her that you would tell her."

I feel awful. That's exactly what I was supposed to do. What I was going to force myself to do before the answering machine message of doom. "Why would you think that? I pretended like I didn't know you."

"I thought you were joking around. I thought . . ."

I am not doing well tonight in the Making Xander Feel Special category. I run my fingers up his wrist and then push our palms together. "I'm sorry. My mom has a history that has jaded her a bit. And I was going to tell her but then everything happened. I'll tell her."

"I think you just did."

I giggle again.

One corner of his mouth lifts into a half-smile. "So is Eddie's open right now? Let's go eat."

Xander leans against his car, licking the last bit of muffin off his fingers. "I didn't realize you had such an in with Eddie. The whole back-door-after-closing-secret-knock. You could've told me this months ago."

"I don't share the few advantages I have." I toss the empty paper bag into one of the trash cans that line our street. When I turn back to face him he pulls me against him. I let out a little yelp of surprise.

He buries his face in the crook of my neck.

"I should probably go. My mom is waiting patiently to yell at me. Better get it over with."

"Is she going to be okay with this? With us?" His voice comes out muffled against my neck.

I trace patterns in his hair with my fingers and smile. "She'll be fine once she gets to know you. I mean, how can she not like Xander Spence?"

"This is true." He kisses me once then releases me.

I start to walk away then turn back. He's leaning against his car watching me go, a sweet smile on his face. I stumble but then catch myself with a little laugh. "Have fun in Florida."

The doll store is dark but the stairs in the back are lit. I take a deep breath and walk up them slowly, not ready to face the anger I saw burning in my mother's eyes. I'm too happy. I don't want my mom to ruin this after-kiss high I'm on. Maybe she'll be asleep. Maybe this will blow over. I laugh at myself. That'll never happen.

The door lets out a whine as I open it. I can almost feel the tension hanging in the air waiting to combust. My mom sits stiffly at the kitchen table. The room is dim; only the under-cabinet lights shine onto the counter-tops. I flip on a light.

"How long?" is the first thing she says.

"A couple months."

"He's the boy you've been spending time with?"

"Yes."

"What about Mason? I thought you and Mason . . ."

I shake my head no. "We're just friends."

She stands to face me. "Where did you meet him?"

I know she's no longer talking about Mason. She's back to Xander. "Here."

"You met here." She points at the floor.

"No, actually it was down there," I say, pointing to the door. Maybe now isn't a good time for a joke because her whole face tightens.

"You know that the Daltons are . . ." It's like she can't even say the word.

"Beyond rich? Yeah, I know."

"Caymen . . ." She lets out a long sigh.

"What's the problem? We like each other."

"People like him don't end up with people like us."

I sigh. "Mom, please. This isn't the eighteen hundreds."

She laughs an ironic little laugh. "The richer you are, the slower time progresses."

I give a fake gasp. "So are you saying he'll be seventeen forever?"

"Caymen, this isn't a joke." She runs her hand down her face. "What will Mrs. Dalton think?"

I stare at her now-clenched fist, my state of euphoria finally gone. "What does this have to do with Mrs. Dalton?"

"You met her grandson in the store. She'll think we're unprofessional."

"I think Mrs. Dalton likes me."

"She likes you as the girl who waits on her, not as the girl who is dating her grandson."

I blink once, the words shocked from my mouth. It feels like my mom just said, "Xander's family won't think you're good enough for him, and guess what? You're not."

"You knew I wouldn't want you to see him and that's why you lied to me about who he was in the first place."

I can't believe my mom, who has been keeping so many secrets, has the gall to even speak right now. "Mom, you're being ridiculous. We have fun together. Can't you just be happy for us?"

"That's all it is for him, though. Fun. Can't you see that? You are just a little bit of excitement for him, Caymen, something different, until he's ready to settle down for real."

"Wait, did I give you the impression that I want him

to propose marriage? I was going to wait at least another three weeks before I asked him about that."

She completely ignores my sarcasm. "He's having fun. It's exciting: date the girl who lives above the doll store. An adventure. But he's not playing for keeps. He's going to break your heart."

"Wow, no wonder why my dad never came to see me."

"Your father never wanted to see you! That's my point, Caymen. Don't you get that? He left us."

I'm breathing hard, my chest rising and falling in large movements and yet it feels like no oxygen is reaching my lungs. "Awesome. You think I can blackmail him? Show up at his work screaming, 'Daddy'? Like Will Ferrell in *Elf*?"

"Caymen, joking about it isn't going to help either of us feel better."

It feels like someone is squeezing my heart in her fist. "*Elf* is no joking matter. That movie is a classic."

My mom lets out a heavy sigh. "I'm here if you'd like to talk about how you're really feeling. And I can't stop you from seeing Xander, but if you trust my judgment or care about my opinion at all, you won't."

She doesn't want to know how I'm really feeling. She just wants me to stop seeing Xander. "Your opinion has been noted." I leave the room hoping I can breathe again soon.

CHAPTER 35

• • • • • • •

Saturday I wait outside the store. My mom and I have barely acknowledged each other all week, and I don't want her to use this occasion as an excuse to restate her horrible opinions about Xander so I'm intercepting that possibility. I shift uncomfortably on my heels (which are actually Skye's heels). I don't wear heels a lot. But there are sacrifices I'm willing to make for Xander, and apparently I can add "heels" to the growing list . . . right after "relationship with mother."

He pulls up in a sleek black sports car and I bite my lip. I had been kidding about him having more than one car. Why does he have to fit some stereotypes so well and disregard the others? It's like he's bent on proving my mom right on the surface so she actually has to make an effort to realize she's wrong. She's not going to make that effort.

He steps out of the car, and my heart lets me know that it still likes Xander, a lot. He looks amazing in a suit. His hair is slicked back tonight, making him look older than he is. His skin has a healthy glow from his trip to Florida.

"I missed you," he says.

"Me, too."

"You look gorgeous."

Even though the dress fits me well it makes me self-conscious, hugging me in all the right places. And the fact that I bought it at a thrift store isn't helping. The dresses tonight are going to be twice as fancy and a hundred times more expensive. "I feel like a fraud."

"Why? Haven't you been to a lifetime's worth of these?"

"Oh yeah, tons." I hit his arm.

"Well, you're lucky. My mom forces me to go."

"She's right to force you. It would be a crime to deprive the world of seeing you in a suit."

He tugs on the bottom of his jacket. "You like?"

"Yes. A lot."

He wraps one arm around my waist and pulls me

close, showering me with an array of scents, from tooth-paste to aftershave. My heels make me stumble a bit, but I lean into him and catch my balance. I hug him and for a second worry that my mom is watching through the window, but his scent and his arms remind me what I'm fighting for. This. Him. It feels good to have him hug me. All the things my mom said about him and me seem to disappear in his arms.

He kisses my cheek. "You smell good."

"You, too."

He glances over my shoulder to the shop. "Are we going in?"

"No . . . no." I hug him tighter. I wish I could take him inside. I wish my mom would get to know him, accept him like she did Mason.

"Okay." He walks me to the other side of the car and opens the passenger-side door, helping me in.

After he climbs in as well, he starts the engine and then gives me a long look. "What's wrong, babe?" Xander grabs my hand and puts it on his knee.

"Is that the pet name we're going with? Babe?"

He backs out of the parking stall and starts driving. "You don't like it?"

"It's okay. It makes me think of the pig, though."

"Are you putting in a request, then?"

"I've always been partial to sweetie, mostly because I'm not sweet so it makes me laugh."

"How about dollface?"

"Ha! Only if you want me to cringe."

"Okay, how about Subject Changer. That fits you well." He squeezes my hand. "Nice try, but what's wrong . . . dollface?"

I sigh. "My mom and I had a huge fight."

"About me?"

"So arrogant. Do you think everything is always about you?"

"What was it about?"

"You."

He smiles. I love his smile. I don't want to talk about my mom. I want to talk about his smile or kissing. I could talk about kissing.

"What is it about me your mom doesn't like?"

"Mainly that you're rich. If you could just change that one thing, it would make my life a whole lot easier."

"I'll work on that."

"Thanks. You're so accommodating."

"So she wants something different for you?"

"What do you mean?"

"Different than her past?"

"Right. Basically she doesn't want me to meet a rich guy, get pregnant, and have the rich guy run."

"She attributes that to his money?"

"I know, it's ridiculous."

"So is that what started the whole living-above-a-doll-store thing?"

I think about how my father's parents gave her the money to start the doll store. "Yes, actually."

"So wait, have you lived there your whole life, then?"

"Yes."

"Wow, she's extreme."

What does "extreme" have to do with living above a doll store? "In some ways, I guess."

"I thought my mom was, but your mom wins the prize."

The ballroom at the hotel is the most beautiful room I have ever seen in real life: big chandeliers, patterned tile floors, thick ceiling-high curtains. Xander steers me toward a table at the front and I take a deep breath. What was that lame advice Henry gave me before I met Mason? Oh yeah, be myself. I wasn't sure that was going to work here. Maybe I could pick someone else to be for the night.

Then I see Mrs. Dalton, and I want to run and hide. Any other time in any other situation and her presence would've put me at ease, but after what my mom said, my hand feels hot in Xander's, like a spotlight is being shone on our clasped fingers.

I stare at her too long because our eyes meet. Sweat

beads along my forehead and I wipe at it. She smiles and waves.

"I think we're being beckoned." He winks at me with his word choice. I want to be playful back but I'm too nervous.

"Caymen," Mrs. Dalton says. "I didn't know you were coming. It's so good to see you. I'm glad to see that Alex has worked his charm on you."

"It was hard, Grammy. This girl wasn't easy to sway." He kisses my hand.

"Most things worth having aren't."

It might just be me, but that doesn't sound like the response of someone who is mad her grandson is dating the help.

"You treat her nice or else." She points at Xander with the warning.

"Aren't you supposed to be saying that to her about me? I am your grandson, after all." He bends over and kisses her cheek and whispers something that makes Mrs. Dalton laugh.

"What did you say to her?" I ask after we walk away.

"I told her that you are fully capable of giving and carrying out your own threats and you didn't need additional bodyguards."

"This is true."

"I'm supposed to mingle for a little while before we sit

down, but instead I will dance with you then we'll find our table."

"No."

"You don't want to dance with me?"

"No, I mean, sure, I'll dance with you, but don't pick tonight, your mom's special night, to be the bad son. She'll blame it on me."

He laughs. "No, she won't. My mom has actually commented recently about how much more responsible I've been. She attributes that to you."

"I didn't realize I was such a good influence on you, considering I've been the queen of irresponsibility lately." According to my own mother.

"Come on, they're playing our song."

I listen for a minute. A live band in the corner is playing some classical piece, and as Lucas had mentioned there is no lead singer. "This is our song?"

"Well, it's your band, remember? So really any song they play is ours."

"So true." Wearing heels makes me the perfect height to nuzzle against his neck. I unbutton the three buttons of his suit jacket and slide my hands inside to his back as we sway to the beat along with some other couples.

He starts making up ridiculous words to the song and singing them badly in my ear.

"You should grab a microphone. The band needs you."

"What? You prefer the smooth voice of Tic?"

"Yes."

He laughs. "Me, too."

A woman's voice cuts through our banter. "Hello again, Caymen."

Xander stops and turns. "Mother." He hugs her.

Then she surprises me with a hug of my own. Her hair is blond and styled. Her eyebrows are shaped to perfection, and she must get something injected into her skin to make it so smooth. "It's good to see my son smiling so much. A smile looks good on him, don't you think?"

"I call it his secret weapon."

Xander furrows his brow. "You do?"

"Mostly in my head but sometimes behind your back." I give Mrs. Spence a sideways glance. I'm being myself; hopefully she isn't put off by sarcasm. She has a smile on her face so I think I'm safe.

Xander pulls me against his side. "Oh well, that explains a lot."

"I just came by to say hello. I can't stay, though. Someone has to run this event." Then she trails a hand down my shoulder. "But let's talk later, you and me. I'd love to get to know you better."

I nod and smile even though I want to say, "That sounds like torture."

As she leaves Xander takes my hand and pulls me close again, swaying with the music. "Now, not that I expect you to remember their names, but let me point out all of my family members."

Not only does he start naming off a lot of people in the room, but he assigns a ridiculous short story to each. "And that," he says, pointing across the room, "is my cousin Scarlett."

"Ah, the doll." I tilt my head. "Yes, she does look a lot like that doll."

"Right?" He laughs, and it's almost as if she knows we're talking about her because not only does she see Xander, but she starts walking our way.

"Scarlett."

She gives him a limp-looking handshake and then kisses the air by his cheek.

"This is Caymen."

"Hello. I've heard so much about you."

I give Xander a sideways look. Does he talk about me all the time? And what is the appropriate response to that statement? "Sounds like Xander needs to get out more if I'm the topic of interest."

Scarlett offers a smile about as wide as her doll counterpart and then squeezes Xander's bicep. "Did you see who your brother brought tonight?"

"No, we haven't been over there yet." Xander cranes

his neck, obviously trying to scope out his brother's date.

"Don't if you can avoid it. Major Cinderella complex."

Xander laughs. "Seriously? Lucas?"

"It doesn't surprise me with where he goes to school." She curls her lip.

Has Xander not told anyone in his family that I'm poorer than dirt? But if he had wouldn't he try to cover up what Scarlett just said instead of sounding like he agrees with it?

"Anyway, good to meet you, Caymen, but Bradley just walked in and I have to go."

We watch her walk away, and I wait for him to smooth things over now that she's gone. Maybe say his cousin is a total stuck-up snob (which she obviously is). But he doesn't. He offers me his elbow and says, "Let's go sit."

He leads me straight toward Lucas and I say, "I thought Scarlett said we should avoid them."

"We can't avoid them all night. It's assigned seating and I'm hungry."

"Caymen," Lucas says, standing and giving me a one-armed hug. "I didn't think you were coming tonight. You thought you'd give boredom a try after all?"

"Yeah, well . . ." I don't even know what to say. I'm still in shock from what Xander and Scarlett just said.

He gestures to a girl on his right. "This is Leah." Leah doesn't stand but smiles up at me.

"Good to meet you."

Xander pulls out a chair for me and I sit numbly.

"Where's Samuel?" Xander asks, looking around. There are two name cards left at the now two empty seats.

"He's on his way."

Samuel arrives less than five minutes later, and like when Lucas and Xander saw each other at the airport, Xander and Samuel hug like they haven't seen each other in ages. Lucas joins in. Next Samuel introduces his date and we exchange pleasantries.

"Samuel," Xander says, putting a hand on my lower back. "This is Caymen Meyers."

"*The* Caymen Meyers?" He smiles big and I'm struck by how different each of the brothers looks. Xander definitely got his dad's darker looks and the others look fairer, like their mom.

"I've heard so much about you," Samuel says.

"I'm sorry."

We all sit down, and Samuel holds up his empty glass and gestures for a passing server who comes and fills it. "So, Caymen, you're related to the Meyers of SCM Pharmacy?"

I start to say no, but Xander beats me. "Yes, they're her grandparents. They're on the guest list tonight." He looks around. "They haven't arrived yet, but as soon as they do I will force Caymen to introduce me."

Samuel continues, "My dad has a lot of respect for your grandfather. He says any man who can turn a profit like that on mid-level stores must be a genius. I'd like to pick the brain of a shrewd businessman like him myself."

I'm too stunned to think. Is this why Xander's family has been perfectly fine with me? He's been pretending I'm rich?

CHAPTER 36

• • • • • • •

"I don't have grandparents."

Lucas and Xander laugh then Lucas says, "She says things with such a straight face, how do you know when she's joking or not, Xander?"

"She's always joking."

Samuel smiles and then says, "I hadn't realized the Meyers had any relatives living around here until Xander told me."

Xander nods. "I didn't realize either, but Grammy told me."

None of this made any sense. Mrs. Dalton must be

confused. Why did she think I was related to these super rich Meyers people? Just because we had the same last name?

I swallow hard and scan the tables around us. Then I eye the door, watching the people coming in. In a way I had been joking about not having grandparents. I do have them, two sets. I just don't know them. My mom's parents disowned her when she got pregnant with me, and my dad's parents paid her to keep her mouth shut. I have the shrewdest grandparents in existence. Meyers is my mother's last name, but it is a common one. My mom can't possibly be related to the SCM Pharmacy Meyers. It's just a coincidence. I stare at Mrs. Dalton from across the room. The sweet Mrs. Dalton smiles at me.

Everyone at the table is looking at me, and I realize someone must've asked a question. A hand squeezes my knee and I jump. I look down and follow the path of the hand up to Xander's shoulder and then to his concerned eyes. "Are you okay?" he asks.

"No . . . yes . . . I just need to use the restroom."

"It's through those doors and to the right." He stands and points then kisses my cheek. "Don't escape out the window or anything. We're just about to get to the super boring part. You won't want to miss it."

I try to laugh but nothing comes out. The bathroom is a welcome relief, and I shut myself into one of the stalls and try to wrap my brain around what just happened. Xander thinks I'm rich. He thinks I come from a rich family. This is why his dad had no problem with me once he found out my name and his brothers act like I am their equal. A sob escapes and I muffle it with my hand.

"Rich boys are stupid," I say, forcing myself to get angry because I can't afford to be hurt right now. I still have to get home with my dignity.

I start to leave the bathroom and almost get a door to the nose when it flies open so fast I'm barely able to step out of the way.

"Sorry," the girl says, rushing past me. She turns on the sink and starts scrubbing at a spot on her white button-up shirt. When I notice her black skirt I realize she must be on the waitstaff. She looks close to tears.

"Are you okay?"

"I just got red wine splashed on my shirt and I don't think it's going to come out." She scrubs harder then reaches for the soap dispenser. "My boss will make me go home."

"Wait. Don't use soap. Here, I have something." I reach into my purse and pull out a little bottle of peroxide solution. We don't get a lot of stains on the dolls in our store, but every once in a while a little kid with sticky hands or a coffee drinker will do some damage.

This solution is a miracle worker. I dab some on her shirt and then blot it with a cloth towel from the counter. "See, look at that. Magic."

She inspects it and then pulls me into a hug. Probably realizing she shouldn't maul guests, she pushes away from me with a red face. "I'm sorry. It's just . . . Thank you so much."

"It's just a bottle of stain remover."

"Well, I appreciate it."

"You're welcome."

She looks down at her clean shirt one last time. "I better get back."

"You better."

She leaves and I lean against the tiled wall. Her "crisis" distracted me for a moment, but it didn't erase what is waiting outside the door.

I have to get out of here. I can't face Xander when I tell him the truth. I head back to the ballroom and nearly trip over a lady with a headset in the hall holding a clipboard.

I start to walk around her but then stop. "Are you the event planner?"

She smiles like she is obviously trained to do to guests, but I see the obvious signs of stress behind her eyes. She probably thinks I have a complaint. "Yes, can I help you?"

"Xander Spence said my grandparents are here and I

can't find them. Could you tell me which table they're sitting at? Meyers." I point to her clipboard as if she doesn't
know where the seating arrangements are located.

"Of course." She flips through the pages, runs her
fingers over a sheet, and then says, "Ah. Here they are.
Table thirty. I'll point it out to you."

"Thank you."

It feels like I'm walking underwater. My legs move in
slow motion; my head pounds with pressure. Once inside
I back up against the nearest wall and she follows suit.

"They're right there. She's in the turquoise top. Do
you see her?"

I follow the line of her finger to the lady in turquoise.
"Yes. There she is. Thanks."

"No problem." The event planner walks off quickly,
probably responding to the tiny voice I heard yelling in
her ear.

Their backs are to me, but the woman in turquoise
has shoulder-length dark hair and the man next to her,
a distinguished silver. I stay on the edge of the room
and walk slowly around, waiting for the moment when
I will see their faces. I finally do. I wait to get hit with
instant recognition, with a feeling, but nothing happens.
A small amount of weight lifts from my shoulders.

The woman looks up and we lock eyes. She gets the
look on her face that adds the weight plus another two

tons of it back on: recognition. Her mouth forms the word "Susan." I can see that all the way across the room where I stand. My face burns to see my mom's name on her lips.

Mrs. Dalton wasn't confused. These Meyers are my grandparents.

The woman grabs on to her husband's forearm and he looks at her in confusion. I don't wait to see how that plays out. I spin on my heel to make a beeline for the door—but run straight into Xander's chest.

"There you are. The appetizers just arrived at the table. It's caviar and crackers with some sort of Greek salad. Do you like caviar?"

"I don't know. I've never had it before." What he had said earlier today about my mom being extreme and the "living-above-the-doll-store thing" hits me. He thinks my mom has done this on purpose. To show me how the other half lives. And I'm just now realizing that in a way she has. My mom grew up rich. This is why she knows way more than she should about the ins and outs of wealthy living. My mom . . .

She lied to me. My life is a lie. No. Her life is a lie. Mine is the truth. We are broke. We are living breath to breath. One extra bit of oxygen consumed could be the ruin of our store.

"What's wrong? What have I done?" Xander asks.

I must be shooting death rays because I'm so angry.

"You only liked me because you thought . . ." I can't even finish the sentence. I'm too angry. Not just at him. At everything. At my mom, the situation, the grand-parents I don't even know. "I have to go."

I whirl around in time to see another familiar face standing there. One I don't care to see. Robert. Seeing his face makes me wish I had poured soda on it last time.

Xander has grabbed my elbow. "Wait. Talk to me."

"I don't think I ever caught your name," Robert says.

"I never gave it," I growl.

"Where is your boyfriend tonight? Mason, right? He's a really good singer."

Xander's hand on my elbow tightens. "Robert, now is not a good time."

"I just saw her at the concert last week. I hadn't real-ized she and Mason were together."

"We're not," I say.

"What do you mean?" Xander drops his hand from my arm.

"They were all over each other."

"No. We weren't." Out of the corner of my eye I see my grandmother about to reach us. "I have to go."

"Caymen." Xander's eyes look hurt, but I'm hurt as well. Too hurt to think. Too hurt to defend myself against his jerk of a friend. I just need to leave.

And I do.

CHAPTER 37

• • • • • • •

I have competing feelings battling for my attention as I walk into the store. One is the extreme amount of anger I feel toward my mom for lying to me my whole life about everything. The other feeling is an intense broken heart that makes me want to rush into my mother's arms and tell her she was right about rich guys and I need her to make my hurt go away.

She's sitting like a statue behind the cash register, like she's been waiting for me. The lights are off with only a few glowing shelves. The look on her face is almost as lifeless as the dolls that surround her.

"I'm sorry," she says. "I've been unfair."

"They were there tonight," I croak. My throat still hurts.

"Who?"

"Your parents."

Shock, followed by devastation, makes her face crumple, and she leans her head onto the counter in front of her. I'm too busy feeling sorry for myself to feel bad for her. I walk by her, up the stairs, and into my room, making sure to shut the door firmly.

I've seen lots of broken dolls in my life. Some with damage as small as a missing finger but others with dislocated limbs or cracked skulls. None of that compares to how broken I feel right now. It's my own fault. I always knew he was part of an entirely different species. Why did I let myself think I could be a part of that?

I change out of my clothes and into some sweats then curl up on my bed and finally let the tears that have been building up inside my head come out in heaving sobs.

There's a small knock on my door and I ignore it. It doesn't stop her from coming in. Why would it? She obviously has no respect at all for my feelings. I push back the tears again and try to control my breathing. She sits on the bed behind me.

"There's really no good explanation as to why I kept

my parents' identity from you. I guess maybe a small part of me thought you would want their lifestyle. That I couldn't give you enough and you'd go look for them for what you thought you were missing."

If she had just left me alone I could've kept it in, but the fire in my throat is ready to spew out. "Why did you leave them?" I push myself to sitting. "What did they do?"

"Caymen, no. They did kick me out. Disown me. I was always honest about that. But I'm sorry. I truly am. I could've been more open. I was angry and hurt and prideful toward my parents. I didn't give them a chance to make amends even had they wanted to. I just disappeared."

"And you made me feel horrible about keeping Xander a secret. You made me feel worthless. Like Mrs. Dalton and her family hated me."

"I'm so sorry."

"Mrs. Dalton knows who you are? I don't understand."

"She knows my story, but I didn't think she knew my parents. She must've been keeping my secret this whole time."

"I just don't know if I can ever trust you again. I'm angry."

"I understand. I hope you can, but I understand."

"And Xander. He's not perfect but he was kind and

treated me well and you didn't even want to give him a chance. He's not my dad. And I'm not you. I'm not going to get pregnant and run off."

She nods. "I know." My mom grabs her stomach and takes a sharp breath.

"What's wrong?"

"Nothing, I'm fine. I just need . . ." She stands, wobbles a bit, and then steadies herself against the wall.

I stand as well. "You don't look so good."

"I should go to bed." She stumbles forward and catches herself on the back of my desk chair.

"Mom. Something is wrong."

She grabs her stomach again and rushes out of my bedroom.

I follow her straight into the bathroom, where she barely makes it in time to vomit in the sink. The sink is now bright red. "Mom! Is that blood?"

She wipes at her mouth, smearing blood across her wrist. Then she coughs.

"Has that ever happened before?"

She shakes her head back and forth.

"Okay, we're going to the hospital. Now."

I pace the hall, waiting for the doctor to tell me what's going on. I've been here for two hours. When he finally comes out I feel close to collapsing. He looks around and

I'm wondering what he's waiting for when he says, "Just you?"

"Just me?" I don't understand his question.

"Is anyone else here with you?"

"Oh. No. Just me." I feel bad. Maybe I should've called Matthew. He should be here. He has a right to know. I make a vow to find his number and call him as soon as I'm done talking to the doctor. "Please, is my mom okay?"

"She's doing better. We're running some tests, trying to rule some things out. We've given her something to help her sleep."

"And um . . ." I don't know how to say it. "Is the baby okay?"

"Baby?" His eyes get wide, and he looks at his clipboard. "Did she tell you she's pregnant?"

"No. I just thought it was a possibility."

"No. She's not. But we'll run a few more tests to verify."

I'm ashamed for the tiny bit of relief I feel. I'm not ashamed for long, though, because with that possibility almost completely off the table I realize that means something more serious is wrong with her. The worry that takes over doesn't leave any room for shame. "Is she sick?" I choke out.

"Yes, and we're trying to figure out what's causing

it. We've ruled out some big things, so that's good." He pats my shoulder as if that will make what he's saying feel better. "We'll know something soon."

"Can I see her?"

"She's asleep and she needs to stay that way for now. I promise to call you as soon as she shows signs of waking." He pauses and looks around again. "You really shouldn't be alone right now."

But I am alone. My mother is all I have. "I don't have a cell phone."

"What number would you like me to reach you at, then?"

There had been many times in my life where I was upset that I didn't have a cell phone like *every* other teenager I know. But now, wanting to just go sit in the waiting room and fall asleep on the outdated couch, is the only time I've felt I might die without one. Maybe I should go to Skye's. But what if Skye isn't there? And her house is ten minutes farther away than the shop. Being ten minutes farther away from the hospital is not an option. I give him the shop number and leave.

I go immediately there and then upstairs, where I sit expectantly by the phone. This isn't going to work. I need to keep my brain busy. There's always something to do on the sales floor. In all my years of living at the doll store, I had never cleaned shelves at one o'clock in the morning. By the time I get to the front window, one wall's worth of shelves is sparkling and I am sweating. I start on another wall. About halfway through the second shelf I find a name plaque without a doll. Carrie. I search the shelves, but she isn't there. My mom must've sold her today and forgotten to put the name tag in the drawer for our next order.

We didn't need to order Carrie, though. She's popular: I knew we had at least two backups of her. She's a sleeping baby, a newborn, with a peaceful look on her face. Everyone loves her. Even I think she is pretty cute, which is a small miracle, seeing as how nearly all the dolls creep me out.

I go to the back. Three boxes with "Carrie" written on the end are side by side on the second shelf. That shelf is low enough for me to reach without assistance so I grab the box down. Right away I know it's empty by its weight, but I dig through it anyway, confirming my belief. I grab the next box down. Empty. I pull down every box, no matter what the name on the end. Soon the floor is littered with packing peanuts but not a single doll.

I now know how long it takes to pull down a whole wall of boxes and search through them. Forty-five minutes. I sink to the floor and put my forehead on my knees. I always thought I shouldered a lot of my mom's burdens, did more than my fair share around the store, kept this place running, but it's more than obvious she shouldered them alone. Why did my mom shut everyone out?

I am doing the same thing.

I grab the cordless off the shelf and dial.

It rings four times. "Hello?" the sleepy voice answers.

"I need you."

CHAPTER 38

•   •   •   •   •   •   •

When Skye walks into the stockroom she gasps. "What happened?"

"I made a mess of everything."

She sits on the couch and pats the cushion next to her. I crawl to her side and lay my head in her lap. She plays with my hair, braiding and unbraiding a section.

"I'm a horrible person. I thought I'd rather die than have my mom be pregnant again. Now I feel like I'm dying."

"Talk to me."

"My mom is sick. She's in the hospital. They wouldn't let me stay."

"So she's not pregnant?"

"No."

"What's Matthew's deal, then?"

"I don't know. Maybe they're just dating. I should call him, shouldn't I?" My head hurts. "I don't have his number."

"Don't worry about it. Your mom is going to be okay. She'll be able to call Matthew herself tomorrow."

I nod.

She runs her hand down my hair a few times. "So where's Xander? Did he run to get you food or something?"

I squeeze my eyes shut, not wanting to think about the other horrible part of the evening. "He's gone forever."

"What? Why?"

"He thought I was rich, Skye. It's the only reason he liked me."

She coughs and adjusts her position on the couch. "Um . . . no offense, but he has been here, hasn't he? Why would he ever think you were rich?"

"Because he knows my grandparents. My mom's parents. And apparently they are some of the richest people in California."

"What?"

"They were there tonight at the benefit."

"Wow. That's crazy."

I push myself to sitting. "It is crazy, right? I should be mad about it. At my mom. At Xander."

"You're mad at Xander because your grandparents are rich?"

"No. Because that's the only reason he liked me."

"Is that what he said?"

"Well, no. But . . ." I run my hands down my face. "But how is either of us ever going to know for sure one way or the other? Even if he claims he would've kept dating me either way, we'll never know because he did know and we can't prove anything now."

Skye takes my hand in hers. "Not everything has to be proven. Maybe you should just trust him."

"And what about my mom? Should I trust her, too? Because she lied to me my whole life. And I'm angry. And I feel guilty for being angry because she's sick." I flop back on the couch and stare at the ceiling.

"I understand. I'd be angry, too. But don't you think they deserve to know she's sick?"

"Who?"

"Her parents."

I nod. I know she's right. "Tomorrow, will you call Xander and get their information for me?"

"You don't want to talk to him?"

I press my palms to my eyes. "No. And please don't tell him what's going on with my mom. The last thing I need is for him to feel sorry for me and come to see me out of guilt."

"Yes, of course I'll get their info for you." She moves to the floor and lays her head next to mine on the couch. "Why don't you try to sleep. I'll watch the phone for you."

"I can't sleep."

"Do you want Henry to come over? He can play his guitar. Maybe distract you for a while."

"It's three thirty in the morning. Don't you think he's asleep?"

She looks at her phone, which confirms the time. "Probably not. He's a night owl."

"I think night ends at two. He must be an early-morning owl."

"Why does night end at two?"

"I don't know. That's usually as late as I can stay up so it must be when night ends."

She laughs and fires off a text message. "If he answers he's awake; if not he's asleep."

"Wow, that's a pretty scientific way of determining whether someone is awake or asleep."

She playfully taps my head. "I'm glad you haven't lost your sarcasm."

Sometime in the early morning I decide Henry is a nice guy. I'm glad Skye was able to see past his pointy nose. I fall asleep to his guitar playing.

When I open my eyes I see Skye across the room on the phone. I go from half asleep to fully aware in one second, springing off the couch and nearly tripping over Henry, who is asleep on the floor. She sees me coming and waves her hand at me, shaking her head. Then she mouths "Xander," and I immediately turn back around and drop onto the couch. Hopefully she's getting my grandparents' info without too much trouble, and then he can completely rid his life of me.

"No," Skye says. "She's asleep."

What time is it anyway? I reach down and twist the watch on Henry's wrist so I can read it. Ten thirty in the morning. Wow. I got at least five hours of sleep. Then how come it still feels like someone bashed my face in with a bat? And why isn't Skye off the phone yet? How long does it take to write down a phone number and address?

"Xander, please," I hear her say. She's too nice. I would've had the number by now. Maybe I should call the hospital while I'm waiting. I look for the phone but then realize Skye's on it. Why didn't she use her cell? What if the hospital is trying to call right now? My anger toward Xander is coming back full force.

"No," Skye says with a sigh that sounds too sweet. I'm about to stand up and take the phone from her when she says, "Thank you," and writes something on the paper she's holding. "Yes. Of course, I'll let her know." She hangs up the phone.

"Let me know what?"

"That he wanted to talk to you."

"Good to know. I don't want to talk to him."

"I know." She hands me the paper and then squats beside Henry, running a hand over his cheek. "Henry. Wake up."

I kick his leg and he jerks awake. "Sometimes you have to be a little more forceful, Skye."

She rolls her eyes but smiles. I say she should be more forceful, but I wouldn't change her for the world.

An hour later I'm standing in the hospital lobby waiting for someone to help me. Nobody had called, but after Skye had to leave for work and I called my mom's parents and filled them in, I couldn't wait around any longer. Finally the receptionist hangs up the phone and says, "She's in room three oh five. Take the elevator to the third floor and someone will buzz you into the wing from there, okay?"

"Thanks."

I'm anxious. I just want to see my mom. If I see her, I know I'll feel better. Most of my anger has changed to worry, but the anger still lingers there and I want it to leave. The moment I'm in her room and see her face, pale but peaceful, I breathe a sigh of relief. I pull a chair to her bedside and force myself to take her hand. "Hey, Mom," I whisper. She doesn't stir.

I don't know how long I sit there holding her hand (An hour? Two?), but eventually the doctor comes in and gestures for me to step into the hall.

"Sorry I couldn't let you see her last night, but we had her downstairs and it's a lot harder to have visitors in those rooms because they're shared. But we had her moved up here late last night."

"So what's going on?"

"We're still waiting on a few more tests. Has your mom been tired a lot lately?"

"Yes."

He nods as if he suspected as much. "I have a hunch as to what's going on, but what we're going to do is thread a camera into her stomach so we can take a look around. The ultrasound didn't show me much, and I'd like a closer look."

"Okay. Is that dangerous?"

"No. It's a common procedure with minimal risk that will hopefully give us some definitive answers."

"Does she know?"

"She hasn't woken up yet." I must've gotten a scared look on my face because he adds, "Which is no cause for alarm. We gave her something to help her sleep that should be wearing off pretty soon. Then we'll talk with her and you can talk with her, and if she agrees to it we'll plan on the procedure for first thing in the morning."

"Can I stay here now?"

"Of course. Like I said, now that she has a private room, you're welcome to stay. You can even sleep in the room if you want."

"Yes. Thank you."

As I'm preparing to reenter the room, I see my grandparents round the corner. Why isn't my mom awake to deal with this? These people are strangers to me. I rub my arms and then give a small wave.

"Caymen, right?" Mrs. Meyers? Grandma? The woman says.

"Yes. Hi, I'm Caymen."

She covers her mouth for a moment as she takes a small breath of air. "You look so much like your mother did at your age." She touches my cheek. "Except you have your father's eyes. You are so beautiful."

I shift from one foot to the other.

The man grumbles at her under his breath then holds out his hand to me. "Hi, I'm stranger one and this is stranger two. Are you uncomfortable yet?"

I give a half smile.

"The only thing that is going to make her uncomfortable is your twisted sense of humor, Sean. He's kidding, honey."

"I know." Could a sense of humor be genetic? I point to the door. "She's not awake yet, but you're welcome to see her."

The woman takes several deep breaths followed by several rapid ones.

"Should I get you an oxygen tank, Vivian, or are you going to be okay? I'm sure there's an extra one lying around."

She hits him on the chest. "Just let me have a minute. I haven't seen my daughter in seventeen years, and now I'm going to see her in a hospital bed. I need to let that sink in."

"The doctor thinks he knows what's wrong and said she's going to be . . ." I started to say, "okay," but then realize he hadn't said that. Maybe she's not going to be okay.

"Caymen," Sean says. "Can you point me in the direction of this doctor? I have some questions for him."

"Sure. That's him, actually, talking to the nurse."

"Thank you. Go on in without me, you two. I'll see her in a minute."

He leaves, and Vivian stands at the door, doing her weird breathing. "You should go in by yourself. I'll wait out here for a while," I tell her.

She nods but doesn't move. I hold open the door for her and that sets her in motion. Will my mom be mad if she wakes up to see her mother sitting by her? After the way she crumbled in the doll store when I told her about her parents last night, I have a feeling she's wanted this for a long time.

My gaze drifts down the hall to where Sean is talking to the doctor. I'm glad to have someone else on my side dealing with the important things. If Sean is as shrewd as Xander and his brothers described then I know he can take care of business.

My grandparents are rich. Weird.

Soon Sean is back by my side. "So how long do you think she needs to work through seventeen years of issues?" he asks, looking at his watch. "Do you think ten minutes was long enough?"

I smile. "My mom's asleep so that will probably cut some time off."

He breathes in through his teeth. "No, Vivian is really good at arguing with herself." He turns to me. "They probably need more time. Have you eaten yet?"

"Don't you want to see her? You haven't seen her in seventeen years."

"I haven't seen *you* in seventeen years cither."

My eyes sting and he gets blurry, but I'm able to blink back the tears.

"I have some time to make up, don't I? Will ten min-utes be enough?"

"I was thinking five, but we'll see how you do."

He smiles. "Ah, so you're my granddaughter after all."

CHAPTER 39

· · · · · · ·

The rest of the day is spent watching my mom go from sheer happiness to anger to tears to happiness again. It's quite a cycle and the doctor doesn't like it. He kicks us all out by the afternoon even though he had said I could spend the night. My mom doesn't fight it, though, which makes me realize she probably needs the rest.

"That went well," Sean says out in the hall.

Vivian shoots him a look. "Caymen, we live a few hours away. Do you think we could stay with you while your mom is recovering?"

"We could get a hotel room if it's too much trouble," Sean adds quickly.

"Our place is really small. I don't know how comfortable you'll be there. I'm sure you're used to much bigger."

Sean throws his hands up. "She thinks we're spoiled, Viv. We can't have that."

"Stop," Vivian says. "We'll be fine either way, honey. What would you prefer?"

I'd prefer they stay at a hotel but that sounds so rude and maybe company would be nice. "You can stay with me; that's fine."

As we walk to the parking lot Sean clears his throat. "So Xander Spence, huh? He's a little too pretty for my taste, but he's from good stock."

"It's not about your taste, thank goodness," Vivian chimes in. "He seems like a really nice boy."

"We're not together."

"Oh. We just assumed because of last night."

"Things happened. It's fine." So this is what having grandparents is about? More people to give you dating advice?

Vivian puts an arm around me. "I didn't want to say it, but he's too pretty for my taste, too, honey."

My automatic defend-Xander-at-all-cost side comes

out and I say, "Once you get to know him he's . . ." I stop myself. I don't need to defend Xander anymore.

Vivian gives my shoulder a squeeze. "It's been a long twenty-four hours, hasn't it?"

"Yes."

I can tell they think the apartment is small. Especially when Sean opens the hall closet door thinking it's going to lead into another section of the house and has to stop with a jerk.

"It's plenty for the two of us and you know we have the whole doll store downstairs, so when it gets too cramped up here, we have room to spread out."

I don't know her well enough, but it seems as though Vivian feels guilty for the way we live. But I meant what I said: sure our house is small, especially when compared to what others have, but growing up, I never felt deprived. I was always happy. It seems only lately I've started seeing everything I didn't have.

Vivian insists on shopping and comes home with more food than we'll be able to eat in a month. She puts herself to work finding a home for everything she bought. Then the dreaded questions start.

"So you said you're a senior, right?"

I nod.

"So what are you going to study next year?" Sean asks

innocently as he reads the label of a can of corn Vivian had bought. It's obvious he's avoiding eye contact because what else would be in a can of corn besides corn? Does he somehow know this is a bad subject for me?

"I'm not—" I start to say, "I'm not sure," but I can't. Not because I'm embarrassed to admit it or because I need to help in the store. After discovering all the empty boxes in the back last night, I realize I haven't been much help at all. My mom has to figure out what the store needs and me hovering is not going to help. I need to move forward. "I'm going to study science. I'm not sure where yet."

"What are you going to do with a science degree? Are you interested in medicine?"

"No, I think crime-scene investigation. But I don't know yet."

"That's a great field to do undergraduate work in. You can go in so many directions from there. The options are limitless, really."

I nod. "Yes, they are."

The phone rings and I pick it up quickly, thinking it might be my mom or the doctor. But it's a man. "Is Susan in?"

"No. She's not. Can I leave her a message?"

"Can you tell her Matthew called?"

"Matthew. No. I mean, yes, I can, but she's in the hospital."

He lets out a scoffing laugh that catches me off-guard. "Is that her excuse this time?"

"What?"

"Listen, tell your mom that if she pays her bills I'll stop calling her."

"Are you a bill collector?"

Sean looks at me.

"Have her call me."

Sean gestures for me to give him the phone and I do. He walks out the door, shutting it behind him. It is nice to have backup.

CHAPTER 40

•　　•　　•　　•　　•　　•　　•

My mom grips my hand tightly.

"The doctor said it's just standard procedure, Mom. No need to be nervous."

"But you haven't been sarcastic with me all morning. You think this is serious."

I laugh. "I'm just too tired to be sarcastic, plus your dad is making me feel so unoriginal."

She smiles. "Do you like them?"

"Yes." It's all I can say. Now is not the time to rehash how she shouldn't have lied to me my whole life. My grandparents are definitely not the monsters she painted them to be. I've just barely managed to keep the anger from spilling out.

"I know," she says, seeming to read my mind. "I stole them from you. I made the decision for myself, but I had no right to make it for you. I'm so sorry."

I squeeze her hand. "We'll make up the time when you're all better. So stop playing sick already. If you wanted your parents back you could've done something less dramatic."

She smiles. "So I'm not going to die."

"I love you, Mom."

"I love you, too, kid."

Sean and Vivian had already talked to my mom so I take the elevator downstairs to join them in the waiting room. When I round the corner I see they aren't alone. I recognize the back of Xander immediately, if by nothing else than his extremely good posture. If Vivian didn't look at me when I came in, I could've backed out without him seeing me, but her look makes him turn. My heart stammers in my chest. I back out anyway and walk toward the front of the hospital and out into the cold day. The leafless trees that line the parking lot look black against the white sky.

"Caymen," he calls. "Wait. Please."

I stop on a patch of yellowing grass and face him. "What?"

"I almost forgot how insecure your stare can make a person."

I wait for him to explain why he's here.

"Okay. I guess I have the floor." He takes a deep breath. "This is me facing failure. This is me putting everything on the line even though I know I might lose. And I'm terrified."

I swallow hard, fighting the instinct I have to comfort him.

"But like you said, anything worth having is worth the risk." He looks at the grass then back up again, almost like he prepared a speech and this is the start of it. "I'm so sorry. That night. The night of the benefit. I was stupid. I didn't know you didn't know your grandparents. And then what Robert said . . ."

"Robert?" The memory of Robert that night hits my mind with a jolt. I had forgotten about him in all the other things that had happened. "I didn't . . . Mason and I were never together. . . ."

"I know. Skye explained. It caught me off-guard, and I thought that's why you were running away. Because you were guilty. But Robert is a jerk. I don't know why I believed him for a second. I should have run after you to make sure you were okay. *We* were okay."

It's true. Robert is a jerk.

He looks down at his hands then uses them to rake

his fingers through his hair, looking less composed than I've ever seen him look. "I understand you were in shock about seeing grandparents you've never seen before, but why haven't you returned any of my calls?"

"You were dating me because I'm rich."

"What?"

"And you can deny it all you want, but we'll never know one way or the other whether it's true or not. Because you can't unknow it."

"I found out less than a month ago about your grandparents. My grandmother told me. I didn't know at first."

"You can't unknow it," I say again.

"But . . ." He wrinkles his nose and then looks up in frustration at the sky.

"But what?"

"Don't hate me for saying this, but . . . you're not rich. I've seen how you live, and when I found out about your grandparents I thought that maybe your mom wanted to make sure you saw how the other half lives or whatever to give you perspective. But when I realized you didn't even know your grandparents, when I found out you were seeing them for the first time at the benefit, then I knew you didn't have money. Caymen. You are poor. And I still like you. A lot."

I let out a laugh and he smiles. The way he's inching forward, I can tell he's ready to put this behind us. But

I'm not quite ready. I still have questions. "But your cousin. She talked about the Cinderella complex and you didn't even say a word."

"My cousin is a spoiled brat and I have learned it's best not to argue with her. But you're right. I did a lot of things wrong that night. I should've stood up for my brother's date. And you. I should've punched Robert so hard that he'd never want to say my name again, let alone use it to get him further ahead. I shouldn't have let you leave. I should've driven you home. I should've screwed the benefit."

"Don't screw benefits."

He stops suddenly, becoming very still. I'm confused. I was sure he was coming to some sort of powerful con- clusion that I really want him to make. Something that'll make me say, "It's okay. Love conquers all." But instead he offers me his lower-lip-biting smile and I almost rush into his arms. For the first time since I walked away from him the other night my heart feels whole.

"Why are you smiling like you've won or something?"

"Because you were just sarcastic with me. 'Don't screw benefits,' you said. You're sarcastic when you're in a good mood. And if you're in a good mood then you must not be too incredibly angry with me."

"You and my mom. You think you have my patterns of sarcasm down, huh?"

"Yes."

"I'm sarcastic all the time, Xander, good mood or not, so there's no need to draw up a chart or anything."

He gives an airy laugh. "Do you know how much I've missed you?"

I close my eyes and draw in a deep breath. There it is. The line that makes me want to forgive him. "How did you know I was here? How did you find out about my mom?" I hold my breath. The answer to this question seems so important to me. Did he decide to come find me after he found out about my mom or before? I so need the answer to be "before."

"Well, when I called the doll store yesterday and Skye wouldn't let me talk to you——"

"I thought Skye called you," I interrupted.

"No, I called you and Skye answered, and all she wanted was your grandparents' information. I begged her to let me talk to you but she wouldn't. So I went to the doll store and it was closed. That made me nervous. I'd never seen the store closed during the day before. So I went to that antique store next door to look for Skye, find out what was going on. She wasn't there, but the owner lady, who I think might be a little crazy, by the way——"

"We use the word 'eccentric' but either one works."

"She told me about your mom. She wasn't sure which

hospital she was at, so I started at Community and then came here." He takes one step forward and gives me his secret weapon of a smile yet again. "Can we hug yet?" he asks, but doesn't wait for my answer, just pulls me up against him. I don't fight it and wrap my arms around his waist. Silent tears trail down my face and I relax into him. I needed him.

"I love you," I whisper.

"What was that? I didn't hear you."

"Don't push me."

"I love you, too," he says. He puts his cheek against mine. "So much."

CHAPTER 41

• • • • • • •

He pulls away first even though I have grabbed a handful of the back of his shirt and clutch it tight. "How is your mom? Is she pregnant, then?"

"No."

"That's good . . . right?"

"No. I was selfish. A baby would've been good news. This is awful. They're trying to figure out what's wrong."

He tucks a piece of hair behind my ear and wipes a tear from my cheek with his thumb. He tries again to back up but I have grabbed another fistful of his shirt. He chuckles and gives up, wrapping his arms back around me. "We'll figure it out. My father knows some of the best doctors in the world and—"

That's when I let go and take one step back. "No. You're not here to solve this problem. The last thing I need is for your parents to think I started dating you because my mom is sick and I wanted your help. Sean and Vivian have things under control and everything is going to be fine," I say even though I'm not sure I believe it.

"What can I do, then? Do your grandparents have a place to stay? Because I'm kind of in the business of putting people up for a night or two . . ."

I smile.

"Are you guys hungry? When's the last time you ate? Maybe I can get some food for everyone?"

I grab his hand. "Xander."

"What?"

"Please don't leave. When the doctor comes out . . . will you just . . . be here for me?"

"Of course." He squeezes my hand and we walk back inside together.

Sean raises one eyebrow when he sees us, probably thinking, *Didn't we all agree that this boy is too pretty?*

"Has the doctor come down yet?" I ask.

"No."

"This is Xander, by the way," I say, raising his hand

slightly in mine. "These are the Meyerses . . . but I guess you all already met at the benefit."

Sean's stare goes between Xander and me, and it seems as though he's keeping himself from giving some sort of grandfatherly admonition. I wonder if that's hard for him, to keep an opinion to himself. Maybe he's learned a thing or two about teenagers in the last twenty years. He obviously didn't have a clue when my mom lived with him.

Finally Vivian says, "Xander, we just met her so take good care of her."

"Of course, ma'am."

"Caymen," my grandfather says, taking Vivian's hand in his, "I'm going to feed this lady. Did you need anything?"

"No, I'm good." I find a chair in the corner and Xander sits next to me. A television hanging in the corner broadcasts the news too quietly for any of us to hear.

Sean and Vivian walk out together. I watch them. How is it possible that one day it's just me and my mom and the next day I have three people who care so much about me?

A fear jolts through me. Is this God setting me up, making sure I won't be left alone when something happens to my mother? I look at the ceiling. *I still want my mom*, I say in my head. *Please don't take her from me.*

"Caymen?" Xander grabs my hand. "You okay?"

"I'm just scared."

"I know. Me, too." He stretches his legs out in front of him and leans his head back against the wall. Then he brings my hand to his lips and rests it there.

I lay my head on his shoulder. "Okay, so detective is out, although I must say that you're much better at observation than I am."

"Only forced observation."

I run my finger along a vein in his forearm. "And no for the music producing? Henry would love you forever."

He smiles. "It would be fun, but it takes money to produce music. For what my completely amateur opinion on music is worth, I think Crusty Toads are really good. They'll do fine. . . . Can we talk to them about the logo, though? Who designed that thing?"

"Seriously. It's bad. But maybe so bad that it's good?"

He scrunches his lips together. "I don't know."

"Okay, so no music producing. That leads us back to this food thing. You love it."

"I do."

"Will you be mad if I say something?"

"Why would I be mad?"

"Because you might not want to hear it."

He sighs. "Okay. Tell me."

"I think your dad might be right about you. I think

you are a multitalented person. And someone who can deal with many problems at once. Plus you have this quiet charm. Maybe the hotel is your future. It fits you well." I hold my breath, waiting for him to get defensive, to tell me I don't know him as well as he knows me.

His shoulders rise then fall. "You're right, I didn't want to hear that."

"I'm sorry."

"But you may be right. I think more about the hotel than a person who doesn't care about it should."

"Caymen."

My head whips toward the new voice in the room, and I'm immediately on my feet when I see it's the doctor. "Yes? How is she?"

"Things went well. The problem is what I thought it might be. She has bleeding ulcers in her stomach."

"What does that mean? That sounds serious."

"It is. And it's a good thing we caught it. It's a treatable condition but one that is going to take time to recover from. Time in a stress-free environment."

"Definitely." Maybe time away from the doll store. I take a breath. "Can I see her?"

"Yes. She was asking for you when she came to."

The doctor turns and I start to follow. When Xander doesn't follow I look back.

"I'll wait here," he says. "I'll fill in your grandparents

when they come back."

"No. Please come with me. My mom will want to see you." I had told her what had happened between Xander and me at the benefit, and my mom seemed sadder than a person who didn't like Xander should've. At the time there was nothing I could say to comfort her, but now that we're together, hopefully that will make her happy.

"Caymen, I'll be fine."

I walk back, grab his hand, and drag him with me. "This isn't about you."

He laughs.

I step into the room alone, leaving Xander to wait in the hall. My mom reaches her hand out to me and I sit by her bedside.

"So I guess I'm a ball of stress."

"Not you, just your stomach."

"I'm sorry."

"Don't be. I wish you would've confided in me more. Let me help out more."

She gives a halfhearted laugh. "More? Caymen, you did more than I had the right to ask for."

I stare at the IV needle in her arm. It's surrounded by purple bruising.

"The store is . . ."

"In big trouble? Yeah, I know."

"I'm working on alternative options. Maybe an online store is the way to go. But, Caymen, this is my responsibility. Not yours. I thought I'd leave it to you at one point, but it's not your passion, is it?"

I laugh then put my forehead on the bed beside her. "I only tried so hard because I knew how important it was to you."

She pats my head. "You are an amazing daughter. You do a lot of things just for me, don't you?"

"That's what family does."

"Caymen, if you want to meet him you have every right to."

My eyes snap to hers. "What? Who?"

"Your father. It's up to you. You won't hurt me."

I nod. I'm still not sure what I want with my dad, but it feels good to have the choice.

"So if the doll store isn't your dream, what is?"

"College. Science major."

"Perfect."

"Xander's here. In the hall."

"I knew he'd be back. How could someone stay away from you for long? Bring him in. I have an apology to make."

I smile. The firm grip my mother has on my hand helps me remember how strong she is. I squeeze back then step out into the hall.

"Is she okay?"

I hug Xander, nuzzling my face into his neck. "How can I feel so perfectly happy when my mom is in the hospital and the doll store is in trouble?"

"Because you know everything is going to be okay. This is like the calm after the storm. Everything has settled, and even though it left destruction in its wake, you know the worst is over."

"Nice analogy."

"Thanks."

"You ready for your after-the-storm talk with my mom?"

"For some reason I'm not as confident as I was the first time I met her."

"You'll do fine. All moms like you, remember?"

He bends his knees, wraps his arms around my waist, and stands up, lifting me off the floor, my toes brushing the tile. "As long as her daughter loves me I can face anything."

"Even redrum? Because after this we're going to your house to watch *The Shining*."

"Now that my future is hotels, is that really a good idea?" I can feel his smile against my cheek.

"Don't worry, you can cover your eyes. I won't make fun of you . . . too much."

ONE GIRL. TWO FATES. ONE CHOICE.

Addison Coleman's life is one big "What if?" As a Searcher,
whenever Addie is faced with a choice she can look into the future and
see both outcomes. So when her parents tell her they're getting a divorce
and she has to pick who she wants to live with, the answer should be easy.
One Search six weeks into the future proves it's not.

With love and loss in both lives, it all comes down to which reality
Addie is willing to live through . . . and who she can't live without.

www.epicreads.com